To Austin, Emily, + Julia,
Welcome to the world of magic and
adventure. Leston now as Wazoo tells
you the story of . . .

"The Wizard within Me"

A Fairy Tale

12/8/2011

Told by Wazoo the Wizard

Wazoo

Written by Arnie Grimm

Arnie Grimm

authorHOUSE®

AuthorHouse™
1663 Liberty Drive, Suite 200
Bloomington, IN 47403
www.authorhouse.com
Phone: 1-800-839-8640

First published by AuthorHouse 4/28/2009

ISBN: 978-1-4343-9774-4 (sc)
ISBN: 978-1-4343-9775-1 (hc)

Library of Congress Control Number: 2009904222

Printed in the United States of America
Bloomington, Indiana

This book is printed on acid-free paper.

To the inspiration of Pat Blue and the continuous encouragement by my wife, Karen Grimm

Contents

Chapter One
The Connection 1

Chapter Two
The Paper Bag 10

Chapter Three
The McDermit Broomstick Company .19

Chapter Four
The Merger between Whitewing Brooms
and McDermit Broomstick 25

Chapter Five
 McDermit's Pursuit 31

Chapter Six
The Brown Family 37

Chapter Seven
Teenage Trouble 43

Chapter Eight
Robert and the Poison Apple 49

Chapter Nine
Penelope Candlewick 56

Chapter Ten
The London Library 63

Chapter Eleven
The Experiment 68

Chapter Twelve
The Love Potion 74

Chapter Thirteen
The Renaissance Faire. 86

Chapter Fourteen
The Tests 99

Chapter Fifteen
Dinner at the Münters 114

Chapter Sixteen
The Hidden Quiddity Potion Shop .121

Chapter Seventeen
JayCee and the Sunshine Command 133

Chapter Eighteen
Oozar, the Wizard's Apprentice 148

Chapter Nineteen
The Séance. 157

Chapter Twenty
What's Under the Porch? 171

Chapter Twenty-one
Which Witch Is a Witch or Not. 180

Chapter Twenty-two
Finding McDermit's Hidden Journal 192

Chapter Twenty-three
My Trouble Has a First Name and It's O-O-Z-A-R 206

Chapter Twenty-four
Jay's Assumption, JayCee's Assumption. 215

Chapter Twenty-five
The Witch's Council. 229

Chapter One
The Connection

Every story has a beginning and an end. But this story started in the middle … in the middle of a town called Broomstick with a potion shop called the Hidden Quiddity. In this shop, a witch or wizard could purchase almost anything needed to do magic.

On the shelves stood bottles filled with the most common ingredients used in making potions, elixirs, charms, and spells. You would not find any voodoo or black magic stuff, as magical law forbade it.

Behind the counter were drawers labeled "magic wands." For beginners, slug-filled wands kept magic from happening too fast. Magic wands for adolescents came filled with spiderweb silk for smooth action of magic. The type of spiderweb silk depended on the type of spider a teenager was attracted to. Of course, black widow spiderweb-filled wands were forbidden for anyone under a half-century old.

The more experienced wand-waver had many to choose from. The most common was dragon scale powder-filled wands, which added a little fire to magic. Then there was the rarest of the rare: a hollow wand that had the hair of a pixie sealed inside. That, my friend, was the most enchanted and powerful magic wand ever made.

Over in one corner were broomsticks, flying broomsticks. The broomstick would be enchanted with all the up-to-date features, like anti-curse deflectors and potion-metering control for precise area coverage. And no one ever resisted the retractable wand-waver.

In front of the counter were the gag novelties. How about a bottle of fire shampoo for flaming red hair? You could have given Willy Wart hand cream to an ex-girlfriend. It was always a good laugh at parties when she used the cream and then passed it around. Instant vomit candy was a huge hit at office parties. Why use fake vomit when vomit candy gave them the real thing?

On a sidewall were the shelves that contained various sizes of cauldrons, pouches, and leather-covered journals with parchment paper pages. Up on the top shelf sat an object of interest to all who came into the potion shop. One tarnished oil lamp had a sign saying "Not for sale!"

Two sisters, Agnes and Harriet Candlewick, owned the Hidden Quiddity potion shop. They both were born in Broomstick. Agnes was twenty-two years old, and Harriet was one-and-a-half years younger. Both were unmarried, and neither had a steady suitor. But Harriet kept trying to get one person to notice her. Agnes and Harriet were witches.

Oh, and who am I you ask? I'm your storyteller. I am Wazoo the Wizard.

The Candlewick family had moved from Salem, Massachusetts, with other families in the 1690s for obvious reasons. One of those other families was the McDermit family, who started the broomstick factory where two broom products were made. One was for sweeping. The other was for flying. Thus the name of the town, Broomstick. Nonmagical families eventually settled in the town as well because they liked the peaceful nature of the people and the surrounding area.

Agnes practiced divination, but she wasn't very good at it. Located in her reading room was a small, round table with a large crystal ball that sat on golden legs that looked like dragon talons. Every day, at a quarter past two in the afternoon, Agnes peered into her crystal ball.

On this particular day, Agnes had only been in the room for a few minutes when she called out, "Harriet, quickly come in here! I see something in the crystal ball."

Agnes was staring at the crystal ball with her dark, mysterious eyes that never gave away what she was truly thinking. The glow of the crystal ball illuminated her thin, round face, causing a reflection from her glossy, Lincoln rose-red lips.

Agnes' shoulder-length hair was dark umber in color. It flowed straight down and covered her ears. She kept it cut shorter because it made her look more businesslike instead of a witch. In the light of the crystal ball, her hair reflected a hint of purple color for some strange reason. Agnes looked out for danger lurking in whatever was happening. She had the tendency to take control of bad situations and work out the problem to a satisfying conclusion. Agnes was always to the point with anyone she talked to. Yet Agnes carried a burden in her heart for Franklin McDermit. She felt it was all her fault that Franklin had emotionally pushed her away.

Already talking, Harriet came into the reading room. "Cloudy at best because the future keeps changing."

"Not this time. The crystal ball went completely dark," Agnes said, astonished.

Harriet was a mischievous witch with a purpose to her pranks. Harriet caused problems that Agnes had to fix. Harriet had good intentions but bad timing.

Harriet had the same dark umber hair as her sister, but she wore it shorter. It hung around her jawline with the ends pointing out. Her bangs hung at her eyebrows, which was just enough to give her spooky-looking eyes.

With her thin and narrow face, she had the alluring look of a witch. With a tilt of her head and her eyes looking to one side, Harriet could hypnotize a man to stop whatever he was doing and just stare at her. When it came to love for Winston Wisestone, her magical attraction didn't quite work. Harriet had a hard time showing her true feelings to him.

Harriet saw that the crystal ball had fully blackened.

"That's not good. Not good at all," she whispered. Her face was just inches away from the ball as she stared into it.

"Just before it went black, I saw Franklin McDermit's face," Agnes whispered.

A cold chill swept through the room, like death itself had just walked into the shop. At that moment, a small group of witches and wizards came into the potion shop.

One middle-aged witch with long, graying hair tied back with an aromatic, tranquility charm said to the group, "Did you feel it? That chill running down your spine?"

Bee, an old witch and a friend of Agnes and Harriet, entered the potion shop right after the group of witches and wizards. Dressed in a multicolored witch's robe and a pointed hat to match, Bee was not very pretty. Glancing around at the group, she could see fear in their faces.

Agnes and Harriet came into the potion shop from the reading room to see who had just entered. Bee was standing in the middle of the floor with everyone circled around her.

She began to speak with aged wisdom, "The power of magic has tipped the scales toward the dark side. Black magic is among us. Be very careful what enchantments and spells you do. For they may do more harm than good. And do not fall victim by succumbing to its power. Death is more sympathetic."

She had conviction in her eyes as she peered deep into the eyes of Agnes and Harriet. Feeling uncomfortable, the witches and wizards left the shop and went in different directions. Bee bought ingredients for a de-aging potion and left without another word. Agnes and Harriet stood still as they watched the old witch leave the potion shop. Bee crossed the quiet street, which was void of any cars in this magical part of town, and winked out of sight in front of the Moonlite and Spiders crossquarter festival glow-in-the-dark supply store.

"We have to find McDermit," said Agnes.

"Yeah, but where do we look?" asked Harriet.

"We wait until something strange happens or hear about unusual events. Then we follow them where they take us," said Agnes, halfway guessing.

Jay and Cindy Münter lived in the quiet town of Broomstick. Jay was the chief financial officer of Whitewing Brooms, which manufactured cleaning products such as vacuum systems, mops, buckets, dustpans, and, of course, brooms. Their sale figures were good, and their stock paid high dividends.

Cindy was an independent consultant to the design department at Whitewing Brooms. She wrote the technical data for new designs of vacuum system products. The latest was a broom vacuum. Each bristle was hollow. A small, powerful motor was in the handle, and the disposable filter bag was biodegradable. The idea was to sweep up the large particles like a broom and then vacuum the fine dust that seemed to be left behind after nearly everything had been swept into a dustpan.

"Drive carefully, but hurry up!" Cindy said in a shrill voice.

"We're almost there," stated Jay, keeping his tone even.

Broomstick expected a new arrival soon. Jay and Cindy were expecting their first baby. In the delivery room, the doctor stood by while Jay coached Cindy. The doctor wore a long, green gown, a scrub hat, and face mask.

Jay was six foot tall. He was strong but built thin. His medium-length hair was groomed and styled. He had a square chin and thin lips.

In the delivery room, he felt helpless. Unlike his job, he wasn't in control of the situation. Jay couldn't help but notice the long, dark brown hair and beard sticking out of the hat and mask.

"Where is Dr. Vandle?" asked Jay.

"He just took ill and couldn't be here," the doctor stated.

It was an easy birth for everyone. Cindy followed Jay's coaching, just as they had learned in prenatal class. The mysterious doctor performed his task as if he had done this a thousand times. And, with that, the baby came into the world. The masked doctor cradled the newborn in his left arm while he held a large, widemouthed bottle in his right hand. The bottle had a rubber gasket lid that was attached with a metal fastener so he could close it quickly.

The masked doctor put the bottle over the baby's lips when the baby exhaled his first breath. He flipped the lid with his thumb to close the lid tightly. Inside the bottle was the collected exhaled breath of this newborn baby.

Before Cindy was brought into the delivery room, her long, blonde, curly hair was neatly brushed. Now after the birth of her baby, her hair was stringy from sweat. Her blue-green eyes were tired and red. Cindy looked up with a plain, pale face and saw the doctor holding her new baby with a glass bottle over its mouth.

"Who are you? Where's Dr. Vandle? What are you doing with my baby?" she asked, alarmed.

Just then, Dr. Vandle walked into the delivery room to discover this unknown doctor holding the newborn in his arms.

"What is the meaning of this? Who are you? What is in that bottle you're holding?" Dr. Vandle demanded.

He was dressed almost identically to the unknown man, but he did not have a face mask. The mysterious doctor handed the baby to Dr. Vandle. Then he waved his right hand with two fingers pointing out at everyone.

"Disrembra!" he announced.

He then vanished into thin air right in front of their eyes.

From birth, JayCee Münter had been an odd little boy. It all started in the maternity ward on that first night of JayCee's life. Something strange happened.

Nurse Florence had been the night ward nurse for thirty-nine years of her fifty-five year nursing career. During the night, she'd change diapers on all the babies. Except on this night, JayCee Münter in bassinet number nine did something very strange.

About two hours into her shift, Nurse Florence noticed JayCee's diaper was on backward. She proceeded to change the diaper to the right way. The next time, she found the diaper was on backward again. Nurse Florence looked around to see if she was the only one in the nursery.

Nurse Florence composed herself by straightening her clean pressed white uniform. She adjusted herself, pulling up on her shoulders and pulling down on her short sleeves. Her thin, straight body held her uniform like a coat hanger. She patted down the sides of her salt-and-pepper hair that she had pulled and pinned back under her nurse's cap.

Nurse Florence proceeded to put the diaper on the right way and used a black marker to mark it with an X. Later that night, she checked on JayCee. The diaper was on backward. The X-marked diaper was in the diaper pail. Then Nurse Florence noticed that all the babies' diapers were on backward. She changed them all and marked them with an X. To her amazement, all the diapers wound up in the diaper pail. All the babies' diapers were on backward.

After her shift, Nurse Florence went straight to the hospital administrator to complain about the practical joke that someone had pulled on her. The administrator reviewed the video recordings for that night in the nursery and didn't see anyone else in the ward that night.

The hospital kept Nurse Florence for evaluations. After two days, she was deemed harmless to herself and others. That afternoon, while JayCee and Cindy were being discharged from the hospital, the administration and nursing department held a surprise retirement party for Nurse Florence. She was allowed to go home under the stipulation that she no longer provide nursing services to anyone.

It didn't take long before the story of the night maternity nurse got passed around the gossip circles. In the *Broomstick*

Valley News, a small headline read, "Good Night Nurse Claimed Newborn Changed Own Diaper."

Agnes showed the headline to Harriet and exclaimed, "This is it, Harriet! We need to find this nurse and ask her what went on that night!"

Agnes and Harriet closed the shop early and went over to Broomstick Hospital to find Nurse Florence. Harriet talked to a young male nurse and found out about the retirement party. Harriet also got Nurse Florence's home address after she gave him a phone number to a psychic reading hotline and told him to call her for a date.

At the door, Nurse Florence said through the mail slot, "I'm not talking to anyone. Go away. Leave me alone."

Agnes and Harriet popped inside and stood behind Florence, who was still bent over and talking through the mail slot.

"We believe you, Florence," said Agnes.

Florence stood up and turned around in shock.

"Let's all go into the kitchen. We'll make some tea and sit down," Harriet calmly added.

Chapter Two
The Paper Bag

Once they calmed down Nurse Florence, Agnes and Harriet learned the name of the baby in bassinet number nine. Agnes also contacted the hospital and had them rescind the stipulation that Nurse Florence could no longer provide nursing services to anyone.

Broomstick Hospital had two very different means of practicing medicine. One side featured conventional medicine for the nonmagical treatment of nonmagical people. "The other side," as the few nonmagical people who knew called it, was staffed with wizards, witches, and magical creatures that cared for the magical community and nonmagical people if magic had caused their affliction.

Nurse Florence was allowed to work in the maternity ward on "the other side." She was happy at least to be working, even if she was in the magical maternity ward with the unusual experiences that happened at night.

With the knowledge of the existence of the magical community and the experience of that night with JayCee, Nurse Florence was never quite the same.

As time went by, Agnes kept searching through various news sources to find any clues to the whereabouts of Franklin McDermit. She looked back about three years before his disappearance and found an interview from New Zealand about missing ice and water core samples from Lake Vostok in Antarctica.

A cargo terminal worker was detained and questioned about the delivery, which was going from Antarctica to the Russian Academy of Science in Moscow. At a news conference after being released from custody, the cargo worker answered the reporters' questions.

"Why did you turn over those samples to this unknown man?" one reporter asked.

"He had the proper paperwork to pick up the crate," said the cargo worker.

"Can you describe the man?" another reporter asked.

"The professor wore a gray robe and cloak. He had long, dark brown hair and a beard," the cargo worker answered.

"You called him a professor. Did he present himself to you as a professor?" the same reporter asked in a follow-up question.

"Well, no. But, ya know, he looked like the professor type," the cargo worker admitted.

"Did you see what kind of truck he left in?" a reporter in the back asked.

"I didn't notice him leaving. I was very busy that day. But it didn't seem to take him long to load up and leave. He just disappeared out of sight," the cargo worker answered.

Over the next decade, things were not dull in Broomstick. Strange and unusual events happened, which were then blamed on black magic. Cindy Münter noticed strange things occurred each time she read a storybook to little JayCee. After reading a story of a snowman that came to life, a blizzard blasted through the town and dumped four feet of snow everywhere. Yet it was the middle of August.

While making JayCee lunch, Cindy thought she saw a snowman looking at her through the kitchen window. When the snow finally did melt away a few days later, it vaporized into clouds shaped like giant balloon animals and floated away. Sitting next to JayCee's bed was a children's storybook about a balloon animal that floated away to go on an adventure.

Cindy read a story to JayCee about a magical garden that had giant vegetables with tomatoes that burst when poked with a finger. In the backyard gardens of Broomstick, tomatoes grew as large as basketballs before exploding with great force. The next year, no one planted tomatoes because seeds had spread everywhere from the year before.

Another time, Cindy thought she heard birds singing musical tunes while she read and sang songs of a fairy-tale story to JayCee. But Cindy noticed that not all the stories she read to JayCee caused strange things to happen. Cindy didn't hear of the trouble after she read about the bear that dreamed about honey or the elves and the shoemaker.

For a while, Agnes was very busy in the Hidden Quiddity with sales of honey blister salve. A breakout of honey blisters was going around in the magical community. When the blisters burst, honey oozed out and covered the unfortunate witch or wizard with this sticky mess. Local bears from the nearby forest had been spotted in the town, which kept the forest rangers and animal control units on high alert.

One early morning, loud banging coming from the front of the store woke up Agnes and Harriet. Agnes got up to investigate and found her shop filled with dozens of elves making shoes. Agnes was still wearing her silky crimson robe used for ceremonial conjuring from the night before. Her hair had a flat spot on the right side of her head because she had slept on the floor in the reading room without a pillow.

Still halfway asleep, Agnes yelled at the elves, "What are you doing?"

Agnes then noticed they were all naked. "Take some T-shirts from the novelty area, and put them on.

After the elves clothed themselves with the T-shirts with a picture of a special wizard on the front, the elves danced and sang; "Now we are boys so fine to see. Why we should no longer cobblers be."

Then they danced and skipped out the front door of the potion shop, leaving a mess of cutup leather and half-finished shoes. Unfortunately, they didn't go away. Magical and nonmagical people spotted the elves around town, causing a lot of mischief. They threw rotten produce at cars and smeared storefront windows with mud. Wanting a horsey ride, they clung on the pants legs of men walking by.

Some nonmagical people mistook them for leprechauns and tried to get the elves to give them their pot of gold. There was a big difference between elves and leprechauns. Leprechauns wouldn't have been caught dead making shoes; elves would never have worn such outlandish outfits.

The elves eventually got bored of causing trouble. One by one, they left the town of Broomstick to seek adventures elsewhere.

Agnes and Harriet kept a close eye on JayCee. After learning his name, Agnes materialized into his parents' home one late night. She quietly opened the door where little JayCee was sleeping. She pulled out a clear, oval-shaped potion bottle from a small pouch attached around her waist. She rubbed the potion into his hair, setting a watch charm around him to let her know if any magical trouble happened.

JayCee grew up quickly. He was skinny with brown-blond hair that didn't exactly lie down. At the crown was a cowlick that had a long curl that stuck out to one side.

When JayCee was five, his father took him to the small circus that came to town. It only had one large tent for its big top. But there were several small tents for the unusual acts, like the bearded lady, the rubber man from India, the half man/half wolf, and the magician.

The magical folks would go to see the magician as if he were a comedy act. But the magician fascinated JayCee. He was dressed like a wizard from a Grimm's fairy tale.

The magician called for a volunteer from the audience and chose JayCee to come up onstage.

"So you want to be a wizard?" the magician asked JayCee.

JayCee nodded.

"Okay then. Hold this bag open," he instructed.

The magician showed the audience a bright, reflective orb. He put it in the bag that JayCee was holding. Then he had JayCee zip it closed. The magician had JayCee feel the bag to show the orb was inside. Then the magician pointed his magic wand at the bag.

With a flamboyant shout, he said the magic word, "Dispera!"

The bag went flat, and the magician took the bag back. But JayCee wanted to see inside. The magician's assistant quickly ushered JayCee to the backstage. JayCee missed the rest of the show.

At home, JayCee put a ball into a paper bag and closed it. He said the same magic word as the magician did.

"Dispera!" said JayCee.

He looked inside, and the ball was gone. JayCee tried the magic trick on many different objects, and all vanished from the bag.

When JayCee went to kindergarten, he carried the paper bag in his back pocket. JayCee made things disappear for his friends. Over the next couple years, things came up missing. JayCee was always nearby, but he was never found with any of the items that had mysteriously disappeared.

One evening, when JayCee was seven, his parents gave a dinner party for prospective investors and top management of the company. The CEO of the company was out of town and asked Jay if he would entertain these people.

A hired sitter kept JayCee upstairs and out of sight. While she was on her cell phone, JayCee went to sneak a peek at the party.

A lady guest spied him. "Well, who is this little handsome boy? What is your name?"

Before JayCee could answer, his father tried to intervene and send JayCee back to his room.

"Oh, let the boy answer," said the lady.

"JayCee," he answered.

"And, JayCee, what do you want to be when you grow up?" asked the lady.

"A wizard," stated JayCee proudly.

"A wizard?" she answered.

Everyone laughed loudly.

"Well, little wizard, do you know any magic?" asked the lady.

"Yes, I do. I can make things disappear."

Again, laughter broke out among the partygoers.

"Okay," said the lady. "Here is my ring. Make it disappear."

JayCee pulled out the paper bag from his pocket. The woman put the ring in the bag.

JayCee said the magic word, "Dispera!"

Then he showed the bag to the lady and everyone else. Applause and laughter enveloped the room. Everyone except Jay was pleased.

The lady said, "Very good. Now can you bring it back?"

JayCee said, "No, I didn't see that part of the magic act."

Jay's face was turning red with embarrassment. With a clenched smile, Jay faked a laugh. "Okay, JayCee, now return the ring back to the lady."

"I can't. I can only make things disappear," JayCee said honestly.

"Make it reappear now, JayCee," Jay said very angrily with his teeth still clenched.

"Reappear?" JayCee said.

"Yes, reappear!" said Jay.

He was even madder than JayCee had ever seen him before.

"I'll try," JayCee said.

He closed the bag and thought, "Dispera? Repera?"

Then JayCee said, "Repera."

JayCee opened the paper bag. Appearing in the paper bag was the ball.

JayCee did this repeatedly, having everything he ever made disappear come back. There was a dirty spoon with dried cereal stuck on it. He pulled out a crystal penguin that his mom had been missing for quite some time.

JayCee was sitting the items down around him as the dinner guests watched and tried to guess what might be in the bag next. Laughter broke out when he pulled out a half-eaten bologna sandwich with the teeth marks still embedded in the bread

A guest joked, "That was my lunch for tomorrow."

By this time, Jay was ready to grab the paper bag for his son when the ring finally showed up in the bag. The lady was rolling in laughter with all the things that JayCee was pulling out of the bag.

"How did you do that?" the lady asked.

She walked away laughing as she put her ring back on.

Jay pointed to JayCee. "Leave."

JayCee didn't stick around for long.

The rest of the party went well, and deals were made. All the time, people talked about how little JayCee could have done his magic trick.

"I counted one hundred and forty things come out of that bag," said one man.

Back in his room, JayCee pulled out the paper bag and put the ball inside. The sitter was still on her cell phone, unaware of what was going on.

"Dispera," he said.

And the bag was empty.

"Repera?" JayCee said. It was more of a question than a statement.

The ball was back in the bag.

The next morning, before JayCee went to school, his father said, "I don't know how you did that trick. But don't ever do it again!"

In disgust, JayCee threw away the paper bag.

Chapter Three
The McDermit
Broomstick Company

In 1692, the McDermit family and other wizarding families moved to this location. The area was secluded and hard to find. It was far away from settled colonies that might object to their ways of life.

The valley had good, rich soil for growing crops. An abundance of water flowed down a shadowy, sometimes hidden creek from a nearby mountain spring. The air was fresh, and the sky was clear almost year-round. The little children of the magical families found nature's fairies everywhere.

The first real business was a broom factory. The original design was made with various types of tree branches imported from the logging areas. To them, small branches were a waste product. Area farmers supplied the broom factory with straw, which included the Candlewick straw farm.

From other colonies, mainly Virginia, hand-braided rope came on large spools. And so went the manufacturing of the highly sought-after broomstick. Magical supply shops ordered the flying broomstick and enchanted them to suit their customers' needs while the nonmagical craft and Halloween costume stores ordered the sweeping broom.

As the centuries passed, products were added on, and the company grew. Still, the original broomstick was being made. Despite improvements and changes to the company, the broomstick was the moneymaker.

Whitewing Brooms sent offers to buy out the McDermit Broomstick, but they were ignored. Representatives came to Broomstick to talk to the McDermit family. Most of the time, the representative never even got an audience with them. On one occasion, the employees made the representative ride a broom out of town. But it wasn't a real riding broomstick.

Whitewing Brooms tried dirty tactics. They went to the logging companies to try to buy all the wood branches to keep McDermit Broomstick from being supplied. There were too many to make that affordable. Then Whitewing Brooms tried to corner the market on straw, but it was to no avail. Local farmers in and around Broomstick only sold to the McDermit Broomstick because of a contract from 1692.

Lastly was the hand-braided rope. But they couldn't find the product's supplier. The spools of the hand-braided rope mysteriously changed hands too many times.

They tried one more dirty trick. They brought union organizers into Broomstick and tried to get the labor force to cause a strike. The employees working the assembly lines for all the products except the original broomstick were actually, through a contract, part-owners of the company. They would have been striking against themselves. But, as far as the other assembly line was concerned, no one knew who worked over there. It was the best-kept secret in town.

No one admitted to working over there either. The union organizers tried to get the government involved, saying McDermit Broomstick exploited workers and paid unfair wages. They wanted the company books audited. Lawyers for McDermit Broomstick presented a document to the employment board, state court, and federal circuit court. Because of that document, the suit progressed up the court system because no one wanted to touch that case. So the ruling went in favor of McDermit Broomstick each time.

Through this process, the lawyers for the union organizer were not allowed to see this document at all. Each time it was presented, it was behind the closed doors of the judge's chamber. Finally, the case was on the docket for the United States Supreme Court in *Broom Worker Union Organizers vs. McDermit Broomstick Company*.

On the floor of the Supreme Court were the lawyers for the broom worker union organizers and McDermit Broomstick. The broom worker union organizers argued they were never allowed to see the document, which was unconstitutional.

"We demand to see this document that is keeping McDermit Broomstick from having an audit of their payroll books for the original broomstick. We have been refused access to this so-called document," argued the organizer's lead lawyer.

The Supreme Court was filled to capacity with the most unusually dressed people that the nine judges had ever seen. The gallery had rows of people wearing various-colored robes so it looked like a graduation from the sixties. Lawyers for McDermit Broomstick requested that all parties meet behind closed doors due to the secrecy of the matter.

"We will allow everyone in this matter to view the document," said McDermit's lead counsel, "with the exception that one section to be remained covered with black paper due to the top-secret security that the United States government has assigned to this document."

The nine judges and two attorney teams were shuffled into a large room with very tall tapestry curtains over the windows. The dark marble floor featured an inlaid silhouette of a bald eagle.

McDermit's lead counsel rolled out the handwritten document on a large oak table. With its large parchment-type paper and black ink, it looked very similar to the Declaration of Independence. It was a government contract that, under its provisions, kept the manufacturing of one, completely spelled out in high detail, broomstick top secret for national security reasons.

The details were kept covered in black paper. The judges were apprehensive about how the broomstick was made or who worked the assembly line.

"That's absurd! A top secret broom in this day and age! This document is so old. Look who signed as president of the United States," a lawyer from the union organizers argued.

Next to the ink-stamped presidential seal was George Washington's actual signature at the bottom of the document.

The judges called in three experts to resolve the matter: Representative Dougle, the chair of the House Arms Services Committee; Admiral Weatherspoon, the chairman of the Joint Chiefs of Staff; and Judge Candlewick, a retired federal judge. The chief justice swore in the three men as certified witnesses. They were given the highest security clearance that could be given. Both sides agreed that the decision would be final.

For three days, the three men carefully read over the details of the construction of the secret broomstick. They noted and conversed back and forth. At the end of the third day, the lawyers and the Supreme Court judges were brought back into the room where the document was rolled out on the large oak table. The detailed section was still covered in black. All of their notes on the subject of the construction of the broomstick were in a box that was filled with a liquid that dissolved the paper into pulp.

In a clean, crisp, fresh Italian suit, Representative Dougle stood next to the oak table. "Under the provisions of this document, the security of this project must be kept top secret and not allow this information fall into enemy hands."

"What?" one of the lawyers said. "It's just a broom made of a wood stick, straw, and hand-braided rope!"

Dressed in his full uniform with rows upon rows of ribbons and metals, Admiral Weatherspoon interrupted the lawyer, "It is not what it is made of that is top secret, but the process in which it is assembled. Neither you nor anyone else in this room will be allowed to compromise the security of the United States by divulging any content of this document to the general public. As a matter of fact, I can have you and your union organization brought up on charges for treason for even putting this document on display through the court system for anyone to hear of it."

Judge Candlewick held up his left hand to calm everyone down. He adjusted his tie, and cleared his throat. "Let's not get overzealous here. But our findings, which is the final word as agreed to earlier, is that this is still a living document and will be observed as a binding contract between McDermit Broomstick and the United States government. If you boys are willing to take some free advice from this old judge, I would suggest you just walk away from this and never mention this document ever again, if you want to keep your sanity."

Not long after that court ruling, Representative Dougle campaigned for the presidency. His campaign was based on national security.

In a speech, he said, "Our national security is stronger than we or our enemy can even imagine. I will supply our armed forces with top-quality water pistols; lead-lined helium balloons; and state-of-the-art, high-powered peashooters. Our troops are totally invisible to our enemies because they wear camouflage uniforms."

That was the last speech Representative Dougle made in public. His last place of residence was the sanitarium located in Witchaven.

Admiral Weatherspoon retired and bought a half-clipper barque and recruited college students for science research of unusual ocean conditions, primarily in the Bermuda triangle. On their first voyage, the admiral found what he was looking for. But he and his crew never returned to tell anyone.

Judge Candlewick went home to his straw farm just outside of Broomstick. Did I mention that he was the grandfather of Agnes and Harriet?

After all that was over, Franklin McDermit's parents retired and left the management of Broomstick Company to him. Franklin was twenty-two years old at the time, and it was ten years before his tragic disappearance that Agnes had observed in her crystal ball.

Chapter Four
The Merger between Whitewing Brooms and McDermit Broomstick

When Franklin McDermit was thirty years old and had owned McDermit Broomstick for the past eight years, he contacted Whitewing Brooms with a merger proposition. He was to meet with the Whitewing Brooms CEO, H.G. White, alone at the local tavern in Broomstick, the Poison Apple.

Behind closed doors in a room in the back, the two men sat at a table. Only the tavern keep was allowed in to freshen up the drinks and keep finger food platters on the table.

H.G. White was a slightly overweight man. He stood only five-foot-six, but he walked and talked like a man much taller. His hair was slicked back, showing his two balding areas on each side of his forehead.

H.G. White looked out of place in a pin-striped business suit in the tavern. Everyone else was dressed in an assortment of colorful, magical robes. Franklin wore a drab, gray cloak. He had neatly brushed and trimmed his brown beard and long brown hair for this special occasion.

Mr. H.G. White started firm. He said, "I don't want a merger. I want to buy you out completely. I need to reduce the competition for shelf space in the housewares departments of retailers."

As H.G. White rambled on, Franklin sipped off the foam of his mug of rich, foamy, carbonated, witch hazelnut soda. He stuffed a finger niblet in his mouth.

He finally said, "Here are the terms of the merger. You get all patents on all products save one, the broomstick. All employees of McDermit Broomstick get preferred stock equal to their percent in the company. No one gets laid off." He leaned toward H.G. White. "I want 75 percent of the profits from the sales of the broomstick. I will keep full control of the production line of the broomstick."

Franklin sat back, still holding a finger niblet in his hand. Just before he stuffed it in his mouth, he finished the terms of the merger, "You will receive all finance reports dealing with the raw materials purchased and all broomsticks sold. I will maintain the document and control of these employees. The McDermit name can be dropped, and Whitewing will take its place."

Franklin stopped talking and stuffed two more finger niblets in his mouth. He took a swig of his rich foamy carbonated witch hazelnut soda, putting foam all over his beard. Then he let out a loud belch that everyone in the tavern could hear. H.G. White sat there, unable to speak.

"Have some finger niblets," said Franklin, pushing a platter over to H.G. White as if he had pushed the deal his way.

"I want to know what is so special about that old broomstick," exclaimed H.G. White. "Why is it so top secret that even I can't know how it is made?"

"If you accept my terms, I will show you everything about the broomstick production," Franklin said, nearly whispering.

He gobbled down one more finger niblet and took another swig of rich foamy carbonated witch hazelnut soda.

"I'm going to have to take this up with the board members and call for a vote of the stockholders. I'll get back with you in a few days," H.G. White said.

He stared at the finger niblets. He wondered if they were real fingers or not. He stood up from his chair, trying for a fast getaway.

"I can't let you leave without this being resolved right here and right now," stated Franklin firmly.

This statement took H.G. White aback.

"You know too much to walk out of here without this deal settled," continued Franklin.

"What do you mean? I know too much?" exclaimed White.

"Let's not act like fools," Franklin said, still talking firmly. "You know about the broomstick. You know about us, and you know those are not real fingers."

Stunned, H.G. White fell back into his chair.

"I ... I ... I'm really not sure I know as much as you think I do. But, if I am right, you are a ...a ..." H.G. White wasn't able to say that word.

"A wizard," said Franklin.

"Yes. Yes, that's it. You are a wizard, and the broomsticks are magical," said H.G. White.

"To put it in simple terms, yes," confirmed Franklin. "Now about our arrangements, do we continue to talk, or do I protect my little secret by erasing your memory completely with magic? I know you have full authority to make this decision."

"Very well then," said H.G. White. "You keep your secret broomstick. I'll have the contract drawn up, and we'll meet again to finalize the deal and sign the paperwork."

"I have all the paperwork right here that we need," said Franklin, pulling out a large parchment and quill. "Just sign here. Then the deal will be done." He pointed at the bottom line on the parchment.

"Okay, McDermit, you win," H.G. White said, picking up the quill.

When H.G. White started to sign, the quill pricked his index finger. Blood ran down to the point.

"Ow!" said H.G. White after signing.

Franklin touched the parchment, and it separated into two individual contracts. "Here is your contract, and I have mine. Now sit and enjoy lunch," Franklin said happily.

The tavern keep and three lovely waitresses carried in platters of various foods. Everyone in the tavern came in and shook H.G. White's hand. They patted him on the back as they said their congratulations.

Franklin nudged H.G. White. "Be careful. Those three women are a tad bit older than they look. It's frightful when the potion wears off."

Later in the afternoon, Franklin kept his word and escorted H.G. White over to where the broomsticks were assembled. They walked through a door that took them to an observation deck with thick glass.

"What are all of these ... these things?" questioned H.G. White.

"We'll start over here with the broom handles," said Franklin.

McDermit proceeded to explain the process of making the broomstick, "The branches are debarked, smoothed, polished, and enhanced with the basics by those elves there."

Franklin pointed at the strange little creatures that were dressed in short-sleeved shirts and felt shorts that were held up with suspenders. Some had beards; others didn't.

"The handles then travel down to here for a wizard's inspection," he continued.

H.G. White recognized the wizard as one of many from the tavern.

"Those stiltskins back there spin the straw on spinning wheels, which turns the straw into gold strands," said Franklin.

Back in one area, a conveyer belt brought straw to men who stood only about four feet tall. All had the same facial trait of a long nose and pointed chin. Their fingers were long, bony claws that picked up the straw and twirled it into the wheel.

"And the spun gold straw comes up over here, where nymph fairies wrap and tie the straw tightly to the handles with hand-braided rope cut exactly thirteen inches long," said Franklin.

The nymph fairies were outfitted in long, white, satin togas. Their exotic-looking butterfly wings fluttered behind them.

"You know, nylon rope would be much cheaper than hand-braided rope," said H.G. White.

"We've tried nylon rope. Ever have a broom unravel in flight? Oh ... I guess not," exclaimed Franklin. "Our staff of witches and wizards test-fly all brooms."

"And how much do you make on these golden straw brooms?" H.G. White asked.

"We make about $91.50 per broom," stated Franklin.

"With all that gold on it, do you know what gold goes for a troy ounce?" H.G. White asked, bewildered.

"Ah," said Franklin. "Our gold is not your gold. It's similar to leprechaun gold. It's there at the end of a rainbow, but it's not."

Franklin led H.G. White out of the building. "Beware of the consequences if you tell anyone of what you have seen. Read the contract carefully on this point. This will be your only warning."

Franklin vanished from H.G. White's side. H.G. White stood alone in front of the Poison Apple with his copy of the contract. He stared at the flaming sign above the two wide doors with wrought iron handles.

Chapter Five
McDermit's Pursuit

All wizards have dabbled in black magic at some point in time. They thought they could control it. However, time and time again, the black magic caused terrible results, and the wizard wound up with two choices. He either gave in to the black magic or fought back.

After the merger was completed with Whitewing Brooms, Franklin McDermit turned to his pursuit. He told no one about that. With the broomstick company out of his way, Franklin turned his full attention to what had been the source of power that made the first real wizards powerful. Franklin knew that some wizards and witches came from nonmagical people.

One story was about a girl who saw a rock fall from the sky. When she found it, it was still hot. The ground around the impact had a strange green glow. The girl went home and collected a cast-iron frying pan and hand shovel. She went back and picked up the rock. The next day, when the rock had cooled to the point where she could pick it up, the girl noticed it emitted a light. She pointed the light at things, and it made them move.

The girl collected the glowing green dirt from the impact and made a tub of mud that she then bathed in. From that day on, she made things move and fly around the room. The girl tied the rock to the end of a long walking stick. She pointed it at things, and they did whatever she wanted them to do.

One day, the girl pointed the rock at a boy she wanted to be loved by and drew his attention away from another girl. She kept him like a well-trained dog, keeping him by her side everywhere she went. He did her bidding for her. One day, the father of the other girl pointed at her and called her a witch in front of the townspeople. The next day, his body was found. Hanging by his feet, he had been tied upside down from the clock tower, dead. The girl had sent her boy to do the dirty deed in the late hours of the night.

After the body was cut down from the clock tower, a rioting mob armed with axes and pitchforks hunted down and killed the boy. There were too many men in the town for the girl to fight off. In the middle of town, the girl was tied to a stake, splashed with kerosene, and set on fire.

An old man heard of a hot spring that healed people when they drank from it. As the old man climbed the trail to the hot spring, he became exhausted and weak. By the time he got to the edge of the hot bubbling pool of crystal clear water, he was gasping for air and clutching his chest. The old man fell over dead, right into the hot, boiling water.

Witnesses said the old man stood up and walked out of the pool of scalding water. The old man learned he could heal people. He also found out that he caused deathly illnesses on those he did not like, which happened more often than him healing the sick. The townspeople gathered while the old man slept. The men quickly tied a noose around the old man's neck and dragged him to town behind a mule, where the local butcher waited. He was cut into pieces and cremated. The old man's ashes were scattered in a secret location.

The stories Franklin came across did not deal with real wizards that already had magical power. He spent hours in libraries. He studied old books and journals with parchment paper notes that stuck out from the pages. In Salem, he rummaged through estate sales for old documents and books. The information from these old documents sometimes led him to someone's house, where they stowed away in an old trunk with more books and writings.

Franklin followed up leads from one document to another. He used the pretense that he was a professor on a historical journey when he asked to look into their attics, basements, or storage sheds. In one shed, he found an old, handmade, thin, dried, leather-covered diary of a witch named Bezzilth Whetstone. He took extreme care when he opened the tattered pages. He read that she came over to America at an early age with her family. They had escaped from a witch trial in England. According to the diary, someone found out about them and tried to collect reward money.

Bezzilth's family tree was described in detail. It went all the way back to the Sorceress Vigoda Whetstone. She bore three sons by a sorcerer named Oozar. The diary said little about him except he was considered at one point to be a sorcerer because Oozar dealt in black magic.

"Oozar," Franklin said aloud.

What made this name different was that, when black magic or dark wizards were ever discussed, variations of this name was always there. There was never any real evidence that he was a real person or where he came from. Some said he came from old Eastern Europe. Others said Asia. The stories started. Osat, Uzora, and Asor, the sorcerer had powers darker than them.

Here in Franklin's hands was a diary that had the name "Oozar," a sorcerer who lived in England centuries ago, even before it was even called England.

"Find something, professor?" a woman asked.

"Yes. Yes, indeed. This diary," Franklin said, showing her the girl's name. "Is she related to you?"

"No. I just couldn't see throwing this stuff away when I bought the house. I felt it might be worth something to someone," said the woman.

"Well, here's a hundred-dollar bill if I can keep this diary," offered Franklin.

The woman snatched the bill. But, as they stood there, dark, mysterious smoke rolled out of the storage shed. As quickly as the smoke came, fire whipped its flames around. It seemed what needed to be found was found. The rest was unimportant.

Franklin McDermit stepped out of nowhere outside the London Library on 14 St. James's Square. He stared at the heavy, dark-stained double doors that had a simple sign above them that read, "The London Library."

Inside, he headed toward the reference section. Under "Oozar" was an English folklore about a wizard who had gone bad. It was in the children's books. Even there, the name was spelled differently, Assar the Sorcerer.

At the research desk, Franklin asked, "Is there a section of reference material pertaining to witches, sorcerer, and wizards that is not in the children's book section?"

"Well, there is the room down in the basement that contains books and journals that were found behind a wall in a northern Scottish castle during renovation for a bed-and-breakfast. But only credited professors with prior approval from the head librarian are allowed to use that room," stated the librarian.

Out of his gray cloak, Franklin pulled folded, stapled papers. "I believe you'll find these in order," said Franklin.

He handed the papers over to the librarian. She flipped through them and saw the head librarian had signed them and crimped them with his seal.

"Well, this is all correct," she remarked.

The librarian escorted Franklin to the elevator and pushed the button for the basement. When the doors opened at the basement level, the rush of musty air met Franklin's nostrils as he stepped out into the dimly lit, windowless floor. Piles of old books with years of dust stood like pillars of a ruined city.

In the far corner of the basement floor was an enclosed room. At the door, the librarian fumbled with old style keys on a large ring. The first key went into the lock with little trouble, but it did not turn the lock. She looked at another similar key. She lined up the key to the hole. She jiggled the key unsuccessfully. The third key went in only halfway. By this point, the librarian was frustrated. She mumbled some excuses to herself as she blew a loose strand of hair from her face. The fourth key went into the lock with some difficulty. She felt the lock in the door move. It wasn't easy to turn, but the door finally unlocked.

"The rules are very clear. Nothing is to leave this room. Press the lift call button when you are ready to leave. The library closes at six o'clock. I hope you find what you are looking for," said the librarian as she walked back to the elevator.

Franklin pulled out his wand and checked for curses, charms, and enchantments that might have protected the room. He failed to do that when he had found the diary and lost other important clues because of it. Remnants of old incantations lingered, but had no power. Franklin concluded the wizards and witches had died long ago.

Franklin sifted through old books, papers, and scribbled notes socked away in the unused room of the library. He read methodically through very old alchemy experiments, not knowing what he was really looking for. Perhaps a tale told through the ages talked about the first wizards and how they came to possess their powerful magical ability.

"Someone must have written it down, describing what happened," thought Franklin.

As he looked through a decaying journal written in Old English with pages detached from the bindings and the cover partially peeled off, he found a piece of parchment behind the front leather cover that was cracking. He slowly pulled it out of its hiding place. He unfolded it and was careful not to rip it. Written in Old English script was the name "Oozar." Franklin only knew a little Old English, as the language was difficult to decipher without a translation dictionary.

A drawing at the top was a Greek symbol for the four principals: earth, fire, air, and water. Franklin carefully folded the parchment and placed it back in the cover. He slipped the entire journal up his sleeve.

He quietly walked out of the room and disappeared from the library basement. At ten minutes to closing, the librarian checked the room and found it empty.

She looked around and thought, "I don't remember seeing the professor leave."

She then notified the library's security of the breach of protocol.

Chapter Six
The Brown Family

Agnes' watch charm around JayCee, which was intended to alert her if magical trouble should happen with young JayCee, soon paid off. But it wasn't anything Agnes had expected.

Trouble happened, but it wasn't magical. The Browns and their thirteen-year-old son, Brian, moved from New York to Broomstick.

Both Robert and Edna Brown were in their mid-forties. They lived in a plush townhouse with the most modern furnishings and a maid.

Robert was a "knight of the road," so to speak. Sales were his forte. Robert wasn't distinguished or debonair. He was a little overweight, a couple inches shy of six feet. His black hair was thinning. His suits were made in Hong Kong. Robert's special talent was his gift of gab.

Edna was self-centered, egotistical, immodest, peacockish, and full of herself. She thought of herself as a trophy wife and socialite. With a slender figure and polished walking style, she had been a fashion model in her youth. But something changed about her after adulthood had fully set in, and no one hired her to wear their fashions. When Robert asked her to marry him, she thought he was her ticket to high society. Edna, as wives go, was a little on the high-maintenance side of marriage.

Brian was a spoiled teenager. He stood about five inches taller than other boys his age. He had his father's black hair and silver tongue, but he had his mother's attitude and personality. He was a bully who had built a little empire at his school. Kids who didn't have much money did things for Brian. He paid a boy to do his homework; another stood in the lunch line and brought him his food. Others waited just to run errands for Brian. Outside of school, Brian socialized with other rich families with his mother and acted as a gentleman of royalty. He knew what to say and when to say it.

Robert looked for a new sales job every two to three years. But it wasn't because he wasn't any good at his job. It was just the opposite. He completed negotiation contracts that supplied products to big-chain enterprises for the companies he worked for. After the contract was signed, they didn't need him anymore. Robert finished his last job where he negotiated a contract that supplied programmed chips with a backtrack antivirus search program by the Slinky software company. The ten-year contract was with the top computer maker that supplied all federal agencies. It was worth billions.

"Here's your bonus check, Robert. Good work," said the human resources manager.

When Robert opened the envelope, he found the bonus check, his last paycheck, and, as usual, a pink slip.

It was by pure accident that Robert had found this advertisement for the sales position with Whitewing Brooms. The want ad wasn't in the regular trade papers that Robert hunted down leads from. The job posting came in a special edition of *Once in a Lifetime Job Opportunity*. There was only one copy on the shelf when Robert picked it up.

When Robert read the job description, it was as if someone had whispered it in his ear. At the same time, it seemed there was a shadowed face made by the words that spoke to Robert. His pulse elevated; the hair on the back of his neck stood up like a hard bristle brush. Robert felt it was compulsory to send his résumé.

At the interview with Whitewing brooms, Robert asked, "What happened to your last sales representative?"

"He retired after seventy-two years on the job," said the interviewer.

When Robert went back to New York, he told his wife and son, "We're moving to Broomstick!"

He didn't want to hear anything from either one of them about leaving New York. That night, Robert and Edna discussed it very loudly. Edna barked out resistance. She demanded outrageous requirements. She even threw expensive porcelain art objects to the floor.

Robert countered each one of her demands. Then he pointed out that, while she was living it up, he flew around the world and slept in airports and motel rooms.

Robert thought, "Moving Edna and Brian to Broomstick is poetic justice."

His final words were, "You can move to Broomstick, get a job using a broomstick, or do what the fashion world wants you to do. You can ride a broomstick in a Halloween costume fashion show. In any case, a broomstick is in your future. Is that crystal ball clear?"

Edna quietly cried herself to sleep while thinking of all the dinner parties, Broadway play openings, women's teas, and fashion shows she would miss. She knew a divorce would be bad. Robert could have easily gotten a job paying $40,000 a year or less, which would have dropped her social status right into the dumpster.

"What kind of social affairs could they possibly have in a town named Broomstick? A witch burning?" Edna thought to herself.

When they arrived in Broomstick, they hunted around for a very nice two-story house. They found one on a nice, shady street with large oak trees and well-kept lawns. Colorful flowers were everywhere. And there were extremely clean cement driveways and sidewalks.

"Perfect," said Edna.

"Awful," said Brian under his breath.

After they moved, they noticed that none of their neighbors drove cars or rode bicycles. In fact, they didn't see much of their neighbors at all. On Robert's first full day on the job, he was introduced to the product lines, from simple normal brooms to Supervac home units.

"What about this antique-style broom?" Robert asked.

"That is our best-seller," said the product representative.

"You're joking," said Robert, laughing.

The product representative just stood there, stone-faced. She said, "Your product line is the new Sweepvac Turbo. Go see Cindy Münter at this address. She will fill you in on the specifications of the product."

That morning, Edna dressed in a navy blue faux wrap shirt with a floral design. She put on a cotton skirt with a ribbon trim. She walked effortlessly, like she was going down a runway, to the house next door. Edna peered around at the neighborhood windows.

The house had an unusual appearance. Edna eyed the front yard. Nothing was out of place. All the flowers were aligned evenly. The grass was trimmed to perfection. She knocked on the nineteenth-century English Gothic-style, oak, carved door. She knocked again. The sound had a deep, spooky tone to it. The door slowly opened. No one greeted her at the door.

"Hello? Hello? I'm Mrs. Brown, your next-door neighbor?"

A voice called, "Come in. We've been expecting you."

Edna entered what she thought was where the living room should have been. In the middle of the room were a large cauldron and three middle-aged ladies. Their hair was pulled back into buns. Each was wearing multicolored, pointed hats with large brims. Their cloaks matched their hats.

"I … I came to see if I could borrow a cup of sugar?" Edna explained.

"Sugar? Why yes. Of course, dear," one of the witches said.

"Are you making a sweetening potion for your son?" asked another witch.

"N-No, a cake, I'm … baking … a … cake," she replied.

"Oh, much better. Easier to swallow, and it will keep for months," the same witch said.

"You don't have a wishbone of a duck by any chance?" the third witch asked.

Edna, not wanting to be rude, politely said no instead of "Ducks do not have wishbones."

She noticed the measuring cup was full of sugar and almost dropped it.

"Well, I have to get going. Thank you for the sugar," she said.

"Oh, don't go just yet. This is almost ready. We would be honored if you would taste it first," the first witch said.

"What is it?" asked Edna. She really wanted to leave.

"You can't tell from the smell, dear?" said the second witch. "It's a de-aging elixir."

"We're going out tonight," said the third witch, giggling.

"Oh no, I … I couldn't. My … my husband will be home soon, and he will want me to look the same," Edna said, trying to make up an excuse. "I really got to go."

She stepped backward to the door, turned, and walked briskly back to the safety of her own house. She shut and locked the door. Her hands trembled so excessively that she dropped the cup of sugar.

Back at the other house, the three witches sampled their elixir.

One said, "I don't think she is a witch at all."

"Funny," said another. "That's what her husband called her!"

Chapter Seven
Teenage Trouble

When JayCee was thirteen years old and in junior high school, trouble with a capital 'T' showed up. On the same day that Robert had his first full day working for Whitewing Brooms and Edna went next door to meet their neighbors, Brian had his first day in a new school.

Not surprisingly, before the lunch break, Brian had already upset the school office staff when he demanded specific class assignments. He disrupted three classes when he showed up late, required a certain desk, and talked out of turn. He was taller than the other kids his age and started bullying right away. He told a boy to carry his books. The boy walked away, ignoring his demand.

Brian was so agitated that no one listened to him that he walked up to JayCee and his friends while they ate lunch.

"This is my table! Get lost!" Brian said to the group.

The group of kids looked at Brian and laughed. Then they ignored him.

"I said this is my table! Scram!" Brian said.

He pulled one of the boys from the bench and pushed him to the ground.

"Now disappear! All of you!" Brian growled at the rest of the kids who sat at the table.

One of the other kids said, "No! You disappear or …"

"Or what?" interrupted Brian.

JayCee stood up. "Or I'll make *you* disappear."

Brian walked toward JayCee. JayCee felt that two fingers were more powerful than just one.

JayCee pointed at Brian and yelled, "Dispera!"

In a flash of blue smoke, Brian disappeared. JayCee's friends stared at the blue smoke and then looked at JayCee with astonishment. Out of nowhere, three supposedly noon aides clothed in unusual-colored robes with wide-hanging sleeves were quickly on the scene.

"Here, children, come with us!" they instructed.

The three aides directed them to an empty gym room.

One waved her hand over their heads. "This event never happened. Disrembra!"

Agnes and Harriet, both wearing matching robes, appeared next to JayCee.

Agnes said to JayCee, "Come with us to the office."

The three went in the opposite direction of JayCee's friends. Agnes found an unoccupied office. Once inside, she shut the door and closed the blinds.

"JayCee, we need you to bring back that boy," said Agnes.

JayCee, scared to death of what he had done, was frozen and speechless.

"JayCee, we are witches and know about your magical power. We're here to help you. Now please bring back the boy," asked Agnes.

"O ...O ... Okay. R ... R ... R ... RE ... Repera," JayCee stuttered.

Black smoke flashed. Brian stood there, pale as a ghost. His hair stuck straight out in all directions. His eyes wide stared straight ahead. Like his eyes, his mouth was wide-open.

Harriet walked around Brian as she observed him closely.

"This one will be tough to charm back to normal," said Harriet.

"As for you, this event never happened. JayCee, disrembra," said Harriet as she cast the spell.

Lunch was over. JayCee and his friends got up from the table and went to class. Back in the office, Brian stood there quiet as the grave. His eyes were wide-open with his mouth agape. He was ashen and frozen. Agnes walked around him clockwise while Harriet walked counterclockwise. Their wands traveled up and down in opposite directions.

Agnes and Harriet chanted together, "Rollie Pollie Ducan Do. Tell us what has frightened you."

Brian's mouth began to move. "Ba, ba, ba, ba, ba ..."

"Well, that's a start," said Harriet.

Agnes lit three candles in a triangle shape around the boy. "Death unshroud and clear the cloud. Candles flicker make healing quicker."

Brian's eyes began to relax. His color returned to normal.

"Sleep like night with dreams abound. Quiet the storm and calm spirits down," Agnes continued.

Brian went limp. Harriet caught him and laid him down on the floor.

"Awake peaceful and kinder, too. Awake to be a nicer you." Agnes paused. "Brian? Wake up. You can go home now. School is over for today."

Brian was fuzzy-eyed. He got up, walked out of the office, and headed home, transfixed.

Harriet said, "We still don't know what happened to him."

"That's true," said Agnes. "And the answer lies with JayCee Münter."

As Agnes kept an eye on JayCee, monitored the strange things that went on in Broomstick, and ran the Hidden Quiddity potion shop, she didn't need any more teenage trouble. Nevertheless, through the mail slot shot, a very queer envelope addressed to:

Agnes and Harriet Candlewick at the Hidden Quiddity Broomstick, USA.

It was from a Penelope Candlewick, who lived in Dragonstep, England. It didn't come with the regular mail. It was written on old parchment paper in black ink. The writing looked like it had been done with quill that had been dipped in an ink bottle. The envelope was sealed with wax and a crest stamp. Agnes opened the envelope and pulled out a letter. She unfolded it and began to read.

Dear Cousins Agnes and Harriet Candlewick,

I am finishing up my third year at school, and I am looking into visiting the United States for the summer. My father will not allow me to go unless I am under the supervision of a relative. I am sure he is really referring to my uncle in Salem, Massachusetts. I found your names on our family tree. Even though you may be very distant cousins, I am sure my father would approve. I am thirteen years old, well-behaved, and mature for my age. I won't be any trouble. Please could you help me?

Sincerely,

Penelope Candlewick

After Agnes showed Harriet the letter, Harriet commented, "She must be a witch from the special school for witches that hold their wands up in the air. You know the type. They'd complain that, when tied to a burning stake, there's not enough wood or kerosene."

"Oh, Harriet, she's only thirteen," said Agnes. "This could be fun for the three of us. I'll send her a next-day express SNARF delivery back."

"SNARF mail, Agnes? Not SNARF mail! Oh, how I hate those little fairies. They are so obnoxious. Your letters show up torn, opened, smudged, and with little notes written on them. Why don't you use Overnite BroomEx instead? At least your letter will get there this year and in one piece," complained Harriet.

Dear Cousin Penelope Candlewick,

My sister and I would love to have you as a guest this summer. There will be the annual Renaissance Faire in which we have our potions booth. We think you would enjoy it and meet a lot of witches and wizards. Tell your father we'll take good care of you.

See you after school,

Agnes and Harriet Candlewick

"You didn't tell her I give out samples of my love potion at our Renaissance Faire booth," exclaimed Harriet.

"Do you really want to tell her father that?" stated Agnes. "After all, that little mischief is just good fun."

Agnes folded up the letter, marked the envelope as next-day express, and slipped it out the windowsill and into the SNARF mailbox.

A fairy pushed her face up against the window. "If my wings freeze off on the polar route, it will be your entire fault."

Harriet looked at the fairy and stuck out her tongue.

Chapter Eight
Robert and the Poison Apple

Robert Brown headed home after picking up the specification book from Cindy Münter on the Sweepvac Turbo. Robert felt excited about his first day at work. Everything on this day had gone his way, that is, until he arrived home.

In the late afternoon, Edna's hands were still shaking from the ordeal of going next door. Edna mumbled to herself about witches and potions while she stared blankly into space.

Brian wandered off after he left school. He took a break from reality when he passed through a peculiar part of town. The unusual store signs and street symbols twisted through his mind like a nightmarish storm. Brian passed by shops that had abnormal names like Astradom Obsession, Moonlite and Spiders, and Big Bang Ariel Haven.

Brian finally got home from school. He was still a little foggy, but he felt good. He opened the door and entered the house. His mother was standing in the entranceway with a bizarre expression that tweaked her eyes and mouth like a fun house mirror.

"Hi, Mom," said Brian in a peculiar manner that wasn't normal to him. "Oh, you spilled some sugar. I'll clean that up for you,"

Brian said. He smiled with an innocent expression. "After that, I'll unload the dishwasher."

Edna stared at her son with a bizarre expression on her face.

"Wa … what did you say?" she asked.

Robert pulled up in the driveway and received the unexpected sight that greeted him. Edna ran out to the car as the late-afternoon sunlight reflected from the sugar sprinkles that clung to her floral print cotton skirt.

"There are witches making potions. Brian's unloading the dishwasher. They're going out on a date. Then they wanted me to taste it. They're wearing multicolored robes and hats. Brian is cleaning up the sugar," Edna rattled on in complete hysteria.

"Calm down, Edna!" said Robert as he gazed around the neighborhood. "Let's go inside so we don't make a scene for the neighbors."

Once they were inside, Robert sat Edna down on the couch. He said, "Let's slowly take this one thing at a time. Start with the neighbors. You were going to go next door and introduce yourself and …"

Edna explained how she used the ploy to borrow a cup of sugar as an icebreaker.

"They were making a de-aging potion in this big, black pot. They wanted me to try it. There are witches living next door," Edna said.

Her hands shook a little. She still had that bizarre expression on her face of the tweaked eyes and mouth of the fun house mirror. Robert looked at Edna's face. He noticed her contorted expression.

Robert, trying to be indifferent, said, "Witches next door? Look, you already have something in common with the neighbors." He chuckled.

"That is not funny!" said Edna. Her face almost came back to normal.

Brian came into the living room and smiled at his father. "Hi, Dad! Can we play catch in the backyard?"

Robert turned to his son, shocked at what he said.

So Robert settled into a much-changed life in Broomstick. Edna mostly stayed inside the house, only venturing out to buy groceries at the other end of town. Brian turned into the perfect son. He willingly did chores around the house. He received good grades in school and never bullied anyone ever again.

Robert himself had gotten five contracts for shipments of the Sweepvac Turbo. He still had a job and wasn't pink-slipped as before. He had gotten used to the strangeness of the neighborhood. He did occasionally see some of his neighbors. He once thought he recognized some of them from the off-limits broom production building.

On Saturdays, Robert and Brian would do yard work. They trimmed hedges and mowed the lawn while Edna planted new flowers in the planters.

One day, Robert saw one of the neighbors and quickly ran over to him.

"Hello, I'm Robert Brown. I know you from the broom factory," said Robert. "Do you work on the production line?"

Winston looked strangely at Robert. Being one of the wizards who test-flew the manufactured broomsticks, Winston didn't answer Robert.

Not wanting to be impolite, Winston answered, "I work for Whitewing in the accounting department."

"Oh, then you must know who I am. I brokered five new contracts for the Sweepvac Turbo," said Robert, bragging.

"Well, good for you," said Winston. "If you will excuse me, I'm late meeting some colleagues at the Poison Apple," exclaimed Winston.

"Is that the tavern two streets over?" asked Robert.

Winston answered, "It is." Then he proceeded to walk on.

After the yard was finished, Robert said to Edna, "I'm going down to the Poison Apple.

"Don't go!" said Edna with a contorted expression. "Remember what happened to Snow White!"

"Oh, stop it, Edna," said Robert. "Maybe you should come along and see there is nothing wrong with these people."

"No, no! I'll stay here," said Edna with twitched tweaked eyes.

Robert walked down to the tavern. When he entered, a strange feeling came over him, like a vegetarian judge at a barbecue cook-off. He sat on a stool at the bar and was mysteriously served dark ale in a mug without being asked. He stared at the mug of ale for a moment before picking it up. On the glass mug was a picture of an apple with a skull and crossbones.

Robert sipped the ale and looked around. Most people paid him no mind. Off in the corner was Winston, sitting with five other wizards. They were all looking at Robert. Robert had seen all six of them at Whitewing, although he had never seen them in any of the offices. Feeling a little uneasy, Robert gulped down his ale and went home without saying a word to anyone.

On Monday, Robert was called in to H.G. White's office.

"I wanted to congratulate you personally on getting those five contracts," said H.G. White.

Robert thought, "This is where I get fired."

"And I want to offer you a promotion," stated H.G. White as he sat behind his oversized oak desk.

"A promotion?" asked Robert.

"Yes, I need a production manager to oversee a very important production line. It will be dealing with purchasing raw goods for the making of this one very important product," exclaimed H.G. White. "And I think you're the man to head up this position. What do you say?"

"A production manager?" questioned Robert. "Well, if you think I can do it, I'll give it my best shot."

Robert felt slightly relieved.

"Good, good," said H.G. White. "I'll have someone show you the production line building this afternoon and where your new office will be."

"Which production line building are you referring to?" questioned Robert, flushed with horrifying thoughts.

H.G. White grinned with personal pleasure as he sat behind his oversized oak desk and looked at Robert like the cat that just ate the canary.

That afternoon, Winston Wisestone took Robert over to the broomstick manufacturing building. After the tour, Robert was ashen beyond any therapeutic help.

Winston told Robert about the warning in the contract that H.G. White had signed with Franklin McDermit.

"Because Mr. White didn't tell you anything about the magical broomstick assembly line and you figured it out enough on your own, Mr. White has you as his go-between. The clause has been lifted from Mr. White's shoulders, so to speak. The burden has been placed on you to keep the secret of the broomstick from the rest of the world," stated Winston with honest remorse.

Robert headed home, pale and stunned. Two wizards that Robert had never seen before met him at his driveway. One wore a bright green robe that glittered in the afternoon sunshine.

The wizard said, "Come on with us down to the Poison Apple to celebrate your new position, Robert."

"I … I got supper waiting inside," Robert said, making an excuse.

"No, you don't," said the wizard as he smiled broadly.

"Your wife is next door here," said the other wizard, pointing at the three witches' house.

"My son …"

"Over at my house, two doors down," stated the other wizard. "He's trying out some new candy from England with my two children."

The two wizards grabbed Robert's arms, and they stepped through a slot in front of them.

At the tavern, they were served platters of finger niblets, barnacle bites, crispy fried spider legs, and frothy mugs of ale. Witches and wizards were crowded in all booths, tables, and standing room that was available.

Just like the first time Robert was at the Poison Apple tavern, Robert felt like a vegetarian judge at a barbecue cook off. Now everyone was looking at Robert. He was, for the first time in his life, really scared to breathe. He was the production manager of a magical broomstick, and he wasn't allowed to tell anyone about it, not even Edna.

Chapter Nine
Penelope Candlewick

Penelope Candlewick lived in the magical town of Dragonstep. Over the centuries, the citizenry of the valley had said that, from up in the air on a broomstick, it looked like the town sat in an imprint of where a dragon had stepped down. Of course, that couldn't be true because dragons had never grown that large.

Penelope was considered to be Proper English. She had grace and manners as well as perfect posture and style. Her auburn hair swayed gently past her shoulders with a combed part on the left side. Penelope's green eyes stared right at people with such drama and magnitude that no one resisted her charm.

A smart girl, Penelope had powerful magical abilities for just being thirteen years old. However, Penelope was never a snobbish sort, even though she came from a strong influential wizarding family. Penelope spoke to everyone as if he or she were the king or queen of England, using only respect and kindness.

Penelope received something very special every morning that she rubbed into her hands; it was pixie dust from her very own pixie. When she touched or hugged someone, she passed on pixie dust, giving the recipient a happy glow for hours.

Penelope had always said, "You can never be happy enough."

Her pixie appeared when she was born. The appearances of pixies were rare. When they happened at a birth, it was considered a sign that wonderful things would happen to that child.

The pixie was only four inches tall. Her hair was bright orange and cut shoulder-length. Her hair covered the left side of her face. Her pointed ears poked out through her hair like little antennae. The pixie had the same type of green eyes as Penelope, as they peered at someone with a mysterious stare.

On the pixie's back were two sets of beautiful wings. The upper wings were yellow with purple around the edge. The lower wings were green-blue with turquoise around the edges. The wings had the texture of fine woven silk.

The pixie wore a green dress made in the shape of a rosebush leaf and unattached sleeves on her arms. Her knee-high suede style boots looked like they were made with grass cuttings. The pixie was as pretty as a monarch butterfly, but she had an attitude of a wasp.

One day, when Penelope was very young, she realized this pixie was with her everywhere she went.

Penelope asked, "What is your name?"

The pixie just stared and shrugged her shoulders.

"Shall I give you a name?" asked Penelope.

The pixie blushed and nodded yes.

Penelope wanted it to be special, so she said, "When a good name comes along, I'll let you know."

Early one spring morning, a sunbeam awakened Penelope.

"Good morning, sunshine," she said to the sun coming in through her window.

The pixie was sitting on the windowsill, watching the sunrise when Penelope spoke. She stood up, turned around, and stared right at Penelope as if Penelope had just spoken to her. She bowed a "good morning" gracefully back. Penelope suddenly realized she had named her pixie.

Sunshine flew over to Penelope and gestured for her to open her hands. Penelope opened her hands, keeping her palms up, to the pixie. Sunshine then sprinkled pixie dust on Penelope's hands and gestured for her to rub her hands together and then rub her face.

"Oh, that feels so good!" Penelope said excitedly. A warm glow encircled her like the morning sun. "Thank you, Sunshine. I feel very happy."

This was the first day Penelope had said, "You know, you can never be happy enough."

Every morning since, Sunshine had given Penelope pixie dust to rub on her hands.

School was out. Penelope waited anxiously to go to Broomstick. A small package came to the Hidden Quiddity from Penelope. It was the things she needed for her stay. Attached was a note from Penelope that said, "I will be arriving the day after tomorrow at eleven o'clock, Broomstick time."

Dragons, for the most part, were wild beasts. Training and controlling dragons was very risky. Breeding them in captivity was forbidden. However, some dragons were allowed to be owned as a form of security animal.

Commodities from dragons included scales, blood, saliva, and unfertile eggs for potions. Only when dragons expired of natural causes were other things available, like their hearts. Eons ago, dragons served as flying sentinels in the olden days of wizard feuds. Wizards used them to fly and attack each other. Dragons carried boulders in their talons. The dragons threw them and spewed fire as commanded. The wizards cast spells with their wands toward their adversaries as they flew in the sky. It was dark times. It was before agreements between wizarding families stopped the feuding. A consortium was established, keeping the dragon population controlled and provided quality dragon products.

Penelope's father, James, owned a dwarf dragon named Whirlpool, who was more of a pet than a security animal. Whirlpool was about the size of a baby elephant. Her scaly tail was as long as a minivan. Her head resembled a cross between a Tyrannosaurus rex and a Triceratops.

James had trained this dragon to do one extraordinary peculiarity. Penelope was ready to go to Broomstick. Penelope and James stood in front of Whirlpool and said good-bye. James stepped back and gave the command to Whirlpool. The dragon bellowed a stream of golden flame that swirled around Penelope. Faster and faster the flame spun until it lifted Penelope up in the air and flashed out of sight. James patted the dragon and fed her a frozen gypsy's kiss, her favorite treat.

Agnes was busily stocking shelves around eleven o'clock when Penelope was due to arrive. She really hadn't given it any thought of how Penelope would get there. She assumed Penelope would show up on a broom and walk through the door.

Suddenly, a flash of light and a burst of heat encompassed the shop. Penelope stood where the swirling golden flame had been a second ago.

"Hello, are you Agnes or Harriet?" Penelope asked.

Standing in the middle of the potion shop was a young girl with shoulder-length auburn hair, green eyes, and a fair complexion. She wore a vintage outfit of the Renaissance era that consisted of a chemise, an outer skirt, a bodice, and a snood.

"I'm Agnes. You must be Penelope."

Penelope bowed gracefully. "Pleased to make your acquaintance, milady."

Agnes said, "The Renaissance Faire isn't for another month, but that dress will be perfect."

"Is that a pixie on your shoulder?" Harriet asked as she entered from the back room.

"You must be Harriet," said Penelope. "And this is Sunshine, my protection pixie."

"When everyone finds out you have a pixie, they will be asking you for pixie dust. Would your pixie be willing to give us exclusive rights to sell some? It would keep you from being bothered," stated Agnes.

"I did bring a thank-you gift for you," Penelope said. She pulled out a bottle of yellow dust from her small bag. "I figured you could use this in you shop." Penelope smiled sheepishly. "It gives people a happy feeling."

"We will definitely need to control the amount of pixie dust we sell around here," Harriet added. "We don't need everyone in town too happy."

"Let's get you settled in. Change your clothes. Then we'll show you around town," said Agnes.

Later that evening Agnes, Harriet, and Penelope headed to the Poison Apple for supper. Walking in, Harriet went over to Winston. From behind him, she put her arms around him.

"Hi ya, Winston," said Harriet.

Winston said nothing, and Harriet walked away.

During supper, Harriet picked up Penelope's teacup and looked at the tea leaves.

"You can read tea leaves?" queried Penelope.

"On occasion, something shows up that I can see," Harriet said, shrugging her shoulders.

"What do you see in my cup?" Penelope asked.

"You will have a great summer adventure with two of the greatest witches in Broomstick," stated Harriet.

Penelope could see the reflected vision of the bottom of the teacup in Harriet's eyes. The three of them had a good laugh that finally broke the awkwardness of just meeting.

Like an older sister, Agnes told Penelope, "Be careful of using magic at this time."

Agnes explained about the crystal ball, the old witch's warning, some of the strange thing that had happened, and the disappearance of Franklin McDermit thirteen years before. Penelope hadn't understood much, but she remembered a story about a room in the London Library and something about a man taking some old book from there some years back before she was born.

Back at the Hidden Quiddity, Harriet told Agnes what she really saw in the tea leaves.

"This is trouble. She is to become a boy's one true love this summer," Harriet whispered, wanting to prevent Penelope from hearing. "Her father will invite us to a family reunion and burn us at the stake for the entertainment segment of the party." But she was uncertain of what was really in Penelope's future.

"You are good at reading tea leaves as I am with the crystal ball," answered Agnes.

Over the next couple days, Agnes wrote Penelope's father about Franklin McDermit's disappearance and a nonmagical family who had a magical boy who was born about that same time. She described the New Zealand saga and asked for information on the London Library story.

Chapter Ten
The London Library

After James received Agnes' request for information about the London Library and possibly the sighting of someone she believed to have been in trouble, he looked into the matter himself. He went to the London Library and pursued the librarian who worked in reference almost fifteen years ago. She was a department head of classical literature at the time James found her.

Miss Abrums told a story of a kindly professor who approached her with a research project that dealt with witches and wizards.

"I told him about the room in the basement that had very old books and papers that were discovered behind a wall in the Blackcraig Castle in northern Scotland during a renovation for a bed-and-breakfast. A group from the Cambridge University science department examined them. Because of how old they were, they built that room to store them in. Only the head librarian's authorization could anyone get into that room."

"Did this man have the authorization?" asked James, like a detective hungering for clues.

"He surprised me by having the required documents from Cambridge and the head librarian," exclaimed Miss Abrums as she recounted the event.

"Can you remember what the chap looked like?" asked James, digging deeper into her story.

"There should be a photo in his investigation file from when he did not check out properly," stated Miss Abrums with assuredness.

James met with Chief Williams, the library security chief.

"Ah, here it is. After another two months, this file would have been deleted from our records," said Chief Williams, who was a little pudgier than he was fifteen years ago. "We're going digital. Anything over fifteen years, we're just offing it. Here. From our security camera is a photo of the man."

From the photograph, James saw a man who fit Agnes' description. He was wearing a gray cloak with long brown hair and beard.

"The next day, a professor from Cambridge showed up. He wanted to know if anyone had been in that room. I told him that a professor was in there the day before, but he failed to check out properly with the librarian," continued Chief Williams. "According to the professor, a book was missing, and it might have been one of the oldest in the collection."

"Can I keep this file since you were going to discard it anyway?" James asked politely.

James knew who the professor from Cambridge was. He was a very old wizard named Lord Banes. He lived in an old house shaped like a stone castle. It sat on an acre of wooded land. Most of his estate had been sold off centuries ago to pay the king's taxes and prevent any enquires that may had led to a trial.

When James Candlewick came calling, Lord Banes was jotting down notes on a spell. The chubby, old wizard sat on a barstool at his polished walnut and marble bar with a porcelain teacup and saucer. His long, wavy, white hair drifted down from his balding head down the back of the purple velvet robe. With his left hand held palm down over the cup, Lord Banes waved his magic wand in a counterclockwise circle. Then he pointed at the teacup and saucer.

"I am trying to have this cup make me a tea and brandy. What is wrong with you?" Lord Banes sputtered at the cup as it exploded into a million little grains of sand everywhere.

After Lord Banes made a tea and brandy the old-fashioned way, he and James sat down.

"I need to ask you about the room in the London Library," explained James.

Lord Banes said, "We put enchantments on the room to preserve and protect those books. We knew of their existence and never thought they would be found. They were very important when we needed to counter black magic. In the wrong hands, those books are deadly!" He sipped his tea. "They are the works of old wizards and witches. They're curses, spells, and potions that used black magic to give them more power. Bad stuff indeed."

Even though the two of them were alone, Lord Banes spoke lower.

"And what of the book or journal that may have been taken?" asked James.

"I felt that something was taken out of the room. I was the last to have a charm on the room. That's when I discovered that several books were moved to reveal the hiding place of a particular journal. Oozar, one of the earliest wizards who embarked into the realm of black magic, wrote this diary. He was a warlock who mastered the power of all magic somehow. He knew more, did more, and caused more harm than any other wizard there was." Lord Banes still talked in a soft voice, as if someone might overhear their conversation.

"According to legend, he tried to immortalize himself. They found him lying on the floor of his castle with his black robe still smoldering with his skeleton inside. His hand held a charred, burnt twig that used to be his wand," whispered Lord Banes.

"Any idea what may have made that journal worth taking?" asked James.

"Maybe it has something to do with his last experiment of black magic, the one that killed him," said Lord Banes.

"The wizard that took it has not been seen for thirteen years," stated James.

"Oh, that could be bad. Truly bad indeed," said Lord Banes.

Assured it was Franklin McDermit who was at the London Library and seen in New Zealand thirteen years ago, Agnes had to find the connection between Franklin's disappearance and JayCee Münter's magical ability from birth. Agnes was desperate for a plan. The Renaissance Faire was in two weeks. Agnes and Harriet promoted their potion shop with a booth that sold potion kits, elixirs, and charmed objects.

Harriet said, "We need to get JayCee to come to the faire."

"And what? Abduct him?" asked Agnes.

"No, we need to have him meet us and befriend him," said Harriet.

"I take it that you have a plan?" asked Agnes, glaring at Harriet. "Oh, let's see. You'll use our love potion on him to make him fall in love with us. Is that it?"

Agnes still glared at Harriet.

"No. Not us. Her!" Harriet said, pointing a finger at Penelope, who was helping a witch with a purchase of pixie dust.

"That is not right, Harriet." said Agnes, staring over at Penelope.

"I told you what her tea leaves said are supposed to happen to her this summer," Harriet whispered softly, preventing Penelope from hearing.

"You don't know who that will be. Pushing them together could be a disaster. Using our love potion to have him fall in love with her at first sight will be a big mistake," Agnes pointed out.

"I'll just give him a smidgen, where it wears off after a minute. Afterward, they will become just friends," promised Harriet as she smiled her mischievous expression.

So Agnes made a pamphlet, charmed it, and sent it directly to the Münter's household, along with a free admission pass for the entire month for kids between the ages of twelve to fourteen years old.

Chapter Eleven
The Experiment

Franklin McDermit had a difficult time deciphering the parchment and the journal. It was a real challenge for Franklin as he translated the words from Old English to modern English, but it wasn't impossible. Some words did not translate well; others had lost their meaning completely. Even with Oozar's immense attention to detail, there were just not enough words in his time to describe the techniques he was using for this experiment.

Franklin was horrified when he finally realized that this was total black magic at its worst. Oozar used this power to perform terrible deeds. He conjured up dead spirits, mixed horrible potions that tormented, and zombied innocent people.

"To what purpose did all this do for Oozar?" Franklin asked himself as he continued to translate the journal.

Oozar's last experiment was incomplete. He had written, "Aet gewinnan ēce biāēd ālibban fēgan ongeador pes mundcraeft aet min swaes drŷlīc craeft."

Franklin wrote down in his notes, "To gain (eternal life live on) immortality (join together), connect this power of protection to my own magical ability."

Oozar described what he was about to do. But he never wrote what happened afterward. Franklin knew this bit of information from the diary of Bezzilth Whetstone. Vigoda Whetstone found Oozar's charred remains up in his tower.

Other than that, Oozar was a mythical story passed down through generations and in different cultures around the world. With all that Oozar had done, his only sign that he gained immortality were just gruesome stories with his name spelled wrong.

Franklin went ahead with his work even after the discovery that all of this was black magic at its worst. Franklin gained understanding of this power and thought he could possibly control it for good magical abilities. Franklin set out to collect the roots of the universe. He arranged to meet someone connected to the Apollo moon missions who had access to the lunar samples brought back.

The sample that Franklin required was from the Genesis Rock found by Apollo 15 at Hadley Rille. The first meeting was at a conference on the origin of the moon. A semiprivate conversation was more about the sample itself and how old it was.

"Could we get together and discuss more in detail what has been discovered about this sample," asked Franklin. "I'll be glad to pay the consultant fee for your time."

This second meeting took place at the Lick Observatory in California. It was secluded up in the hills overlooking San Jose.

Franklin suggested, "What if I told you that I have an experiment that would break down the sample to its most elementary property, the Infusionary. The particle/wave that lies between energy and matter that determines what element will be formed."

The scientist was a thin, middle-aged man with short hair that wasn't cut well. His mustache hung over his upper lip. He wasn't entirely sure why the meeting was way out of the way of any learning institute. It made him nervous. As the two stood outside looking at the view, the scientist listened intently to Franklin's explanation of the experiment.

"I never heard of this kind of technology," stated the scientist. "What university is this laboratory at?"

Franklin skirted the question by divulging his secret plan to keep the information quiet from unscrupulous government spies who would use this technology to invent new doomsday weapons.

"In a Swiss safety deposit box, you will find all the proper documents and the account number for the five million dollars," said Franklin. "All you need to do is put the rock sample in the box."

Franklin slid a small key card over to the scientist.

The Genesis solar wind recovery capsule with its cargo on board streaked through the Earth's atmosphere and headed for the Utah landing site. The parachute charges went off as scheduled. The parachutes deployed to slow down the capsule for a soft landing. But something went wrong. The parachutes tangled around each other, and the capsule headed off course to a crash landing.

A man wearing a gray cloak with long, dark brown hair and beard stood nearby with a wand pointed directly at the Genesis recovery capsule. The capsule slammed into the earth, causing a cloud of dust to engulf the impact area. Franklin McDermit quickly collected some of the solar wind sample pods and escaped without a trace.

In New Zealand were ice and water core samples from Lake Vostok in Antarctica, heading toward the Russian Academy of Science in Moscow. Franklin handed over paperwork to the cargo terminal worker and picked up the samples. When the cargo worker had been satisfied that the paperwork was in order, he stamped all the copies and kept one copy for his records.

With the ice and water from Antarctica safely stored in a transport container that was normally used to bring raw material to the broomstick factory magically, the container and Franklin disappeared from the cargo terminal in New Zealand.

With all the necessary ingredients assembled, Franklin set up a hidden laboratory site in a cavern just outside of Broomstick. A makeshift worktable sat up against one side of the far wall of the last cavern room. On the table sat the bottles with the three purified elements of earth, fire, and, water needed for the experiment. The parchment sat next to a hollowed-out wand made of two pieces that screwed together in the middle.

Written on a notepad on top of the parchment were the words, "Change the element of wind from dying man's breath to clean, pure baby's first breath. This should create white magic power."

Franklin showed up at the secluded cavern, still dressed in the long green gown, a scrub hat, and face mask, still carefully clutching the bottle of newborn baby's first breath from JayCee Münter.

Franklin went right to work. Beakers and hoses bubbled with the elements as they combined. Gases and liquids churned and coagulated. A ghostly image seemed to have appeared at the edge of one glass cylinder. Franklin leaned over a large cauldron, mumbling incantations as the elements flowed from a large, clear tube into the cauldron. Franklin slowly waved his wand counterclockwise. Inside the cauldron, the deep violet concoction bubbled, swirled, and splashed like a storm at sea.

A vortex opened within the mist of brilliant blue flames as it swirled. The center of the vortex was darker than the sky of a planet that circled a dead star. It was blacker than pools of tar that trapped its unsuspecting prey. Franklin felt the emptiness inside the center of the vortex. It felt to him as though the universe had never existed.

From the workbench, Franklin took the two pieces of the hollow wand. He used both hands, immersed the wand segments into the vortex, and screwed the halves together. Trapped inside the wand was a piece of what the vortex held so tightly.

Franklin pulled out the wand from the vortex with his right hand. Franklin realized he was unable to pull his other hand out. Something had grabbed a hold of his left hand. Franklin struggled to get free of the vortex. He dropped the newly made wand on the floor and grabbed onto the side of the cauldron. Franklin knocked his own wand off the workbench as he was pulled into the cauldron headfirst. The cauldron imploded into itself. The vortex collapsed closed, leaving a charred circle on the cavern floor.

Sitting on a small, round table was a crystal ball with golden dragon talons. A young witch was staring into the crystal ball.

She was the only witness to this tragic event as Franklin McDermit disappeared into the vortex on the same day that JayCee Münter was born.

"Harriet, quickly come in here! I see something in the crystal ball." Agnes called out.

Chapter Twelve
The Love Potion

Austin and Marlin Hallmark were brothers who grew up in Broomstick. Their parents had worked for McDermit Broomstick and stayed on when it became Whitewing Brooms. They were not a wizarding family. The Hallmark family was as magical as a magician in a carnival. They knew of the unusual side to Broomstick, but the Hallmarks ignored it as if it wasn't there.

Austin was older of the two, but not by much. Ten months separated their ages. At the age of sixteen and fifteen, the two brothers were best of friends, which was unusual for brothers. Austin had sandy hair, a farmer's tan complexion, and an average-featured face. Marlin was the serious one of the two. Marlin was committed to detail in everything he did. No one mistook Marlin for Austin, even though the two passed as twins at first glance.

Austin and Marlin raised pigs for the Renaissance Faire livestock competition. For three years running, they had won first prize for their pigs due to Marlin's attention to detail.

A plain-looking girl with dull gray eyes had taken a liking to Austin a few years back, but Austin didn't notice her. She was skinny with stringy, black hair that she would keep tied back.

Wanda Whetstone came from a different part of town, making it hard to get Austin to notice her when they would only cross paths at the Renaissance Faire.

For the past three years, Wanda had hung around the barn area and watched Austin as he cleaned the pigs for the competition. Austin hadn't paid any attention to Wanda because he had been too busy with the pigs. Wanda changed all that on this particular Renaissance Faire, the same year that Agnes and Harriet needed to befriend JayCee.

Marlin did notice Wanda each year as she stood around and watched Austin. Wanda would make him feel very uncomfortable, as her cold, gray eyes looked like two gravestones staring at him.

Wanda was now seventeen years old, and she had changed from that skinny, little girl to a smoothed-out, slender young woman with very long, shiny, coal black hair and gray eyes that showed alluring, mystical power. She wore a Renaissance-style outfit with a tightly tied bodice.

Austin had just stepped out of the pig barn when Wanda stepped in front of him and offered him a chocolate parfait. That was all it took for Austin to finally notice her. Marlin witnessed the change in Austin on that day. They lost the competition because Austin went with Wanda after he ate the chocolate parfait. Marlin couldn't get the pigs ready by himself in time for the judging. He felt so bitter that he wanted to kill his brother. Austin acted strangely when he came home after being out late that night. Marlin covered for Austin so he didn't get into trouble with their parents because Austin missed dinner.

Austin neglected his responsibilities around the farm. He stayed out late, ignored the animals, and stopped eating at home. After Austin came in late one night, Marlin pushed him down to the ground.

"What has gotten into you? Can't you see this girl is ruining your life?" yelled Marlin.

Austin replied, "Leave me alone! I know what I'm doing!"

Marlin tracked down where Wanda lived and found out much more than he wanted to know. He had accidentally stumbled into the magical world of Broomstick. Marlin found himself surrounded by witches and wizards. Everywhere Marlin turned, he saw all kinds of magical shops—clothing stores, potions supplies, antiquity stores, healing clinics, and clairvoyant parlors. This was the world of Wanda Whetstone. Wanda Whetstone was a witch.

Deep down, Marlin felt demonophobia setting in. He was frozen with fear with no solution. Marlin was faced with finding someone he could trust to help who wouldn't think he was off his rocker.

Marlin remembered one person from the Renaissance Faire that could help him. He looked up a woman, Madam Olga, who was part of the gypsy camp at the Renaissance Faire that told fortunes.

Marlin looked through Broomstick for her. But she wasn't among the gypsy fortune-tellers in town. Madam Olga traveled with a gypsy camp from one faire to another. But she wasn't a witch, and she didn't really have any magical powers. She was knowledgeable in the occult of magic.

Marlin found the gypsy camp just outside the town of Shadow Creek. The sun had just set, and Marlin heard the music begin to play. Violins, mandolins, and tambourines echoed in the air as Marlin cautiously approached the gypsy camp. Marlin peered through the bushes and looked at the circle of wagons. He saw the fortune-teller as she sat by her wagon.

Madam Olga was a woman in her later years with graying hair pulled back into a bun. She wore a brightly colored bandana around her head. She was wearing a dress with a scarf type skirt made from old scraps of cloth. Around her waist were a sequined sash and a leather belt.

Marlin was grabbed by his shirt from behind. He noticed his attacker was wearing a forest green velour vest over a white shirt that laced up the front and brown velour pants.

"You seek a gypsy good time, my friend?" asked the dark-haired gypsy man.

"No, no. I was just—" Marlin started to say. "I need to talk to Madam Olga."

"She is not available for fortune-telling now. Come and see her at the faire next week," stated the man.

"I'm … my brother is in trouble. I need Madam Olga's help," pleaded Marlin.

The man asked, "What kind of trouble?"

"A witch has bewitched my brother," said Marlin.

A stern expression molded into the gypsy man's face. Without another word, he escorted Marlin into the gypsy camp, where the music had been playing and the gypsy girls were dancing around the campfire. The music stopped suddenly as everyone turned toward Marlin and the man. The man directed Marlin to go inside Madam Olga's wagon and wait.

Madam Olga came into her wagon, shut the door, and sat down on the other side of the table where Marlin was sitting. Madam Olga shuffled and then began to view tarot cards one at a time.

She peered up from the tarot cards. "Yes, I can help you. First, you'll need a lock of her hair and piece of her clothing. Return to me with these items. Then and only then can I help you and your brother."

This wasn't an easy task. It took several weeks of failed attempts to follow Austin to where he would meet Wanda in the evenings. Strange happenings occurred. Many times, Austin had turned street corners and vanished from Marlin's sight. Other times, Marlin found he had walked right into a blind alley with no way out.

On this one particular night, Marlin kept back far enough that he didn't have any eerie happenings occur. He followed Austin down a dimly lit street without any vehicle traffic to speak of. Austin walked up to a building with a rounded log front and double-wide wooden doors with wrought iron handles. Above the doors, in what seemed to be small jets of fire, was a burning sign.

Marlin felt a knot in his stomach as he read the sign slowly, "Poison Apple Tavern."

He thought to himself, "This makes perfect sense."

Marlin grabbed a hold of the wrought iron door handle with sweaty palms and pulled open the door just enough to slip in. Marlin stood behind other people and took a seat near, but not within eyesight, of his brother and Wanda. Marlin felt queasy as he sat there. It was a strange feeling, like being the guest of honor at a human sacrifice ritual. He waited for the right moment and worked up his courage to make his way over toward the two of them as Austin and Wanda sat in a booth.

Austin and Wanda sat on the same side of the table with their backs toward the doors. Wanda was on the outside, facing Austin while he stared with glassy eyes into her pupils.

With scissors in hand, Marlin sat in the booth right behind them. He had the opportunity to first snip a piece of Wanda's hair. Her straight black hair had draped over the half wall between the booths, landing right next to Marlin's neck. With sweat beading up on his forehead, Marlin cut her hair. His hand trembled as the sharp edges sliced through the coal-colored strands. Marlin then got down under the table and gently tugged on her long skirt. He cut part of her hem away from her long skirt. Marlin sat back up in the booth. Sweat rolled down the side of his face. Large wet circles formed under his underarms. The tavern keep noticed Marlin acting strangely and walked over to him.

"What are you up to?" he asked.

"Nothing," said Marlin.

He quickly stood up and exited the tavern without looking back.

Marlin caught up with Madam Olga halfway across the state at a county fair. When evening had come, Marlin was once again in her wagon. He set down the hair and cloth swatch from Wanda.

"This isn't going to—" Marlin said, hesitating.

Madam Olga finished what Marlin couldn't say. "No, it will not kill her."

Madam Olga wrapped the hair inside the cloth swatch and tied it together with thread from handwoven rope that she had removed from a witch's flying broom. She held it over the flame from a white, blue, and green wax candle until the hair began to singe and the cloth caught on fire. She set down the flaming cloth and hair in a plate and allowed it to burn completely.

Madam Olga looked at Marlin. "Go to your brother. The spell has been broken."

In that moment, Wanda knew what had just happened. She saw it in Austin's eyes. Austin felt the change. To him, it was as if he woke up from a never-ending dream.

"Let me out," said Austin to Wanda as he attempted to stand up from their usual corner booth at the Poison Apple.

Furious with himself for the time he had wasted, Austin walked from the Poison Apple and headed through the strange store district that was clear across to the other side of town before he caught a bus that took him close to home.

When Marlin got home, he tried to talk to Austin, who had already returned to the farm. He was working inside the barn on the neglected wagon. But Marlin found Austin unsociable and uncooperative. Austin felt sour, betrayed by both his brother and Wanda.

The next day, Wanda came to the Hallmark farm after Marlin got home. Her intentions were to set things right. She wanted Austin back. It was obvious to Wanda what Marlin had done when she realized her hair and dress had been cut. There was no second chance with a spell. Austin was pervious to any of her magic.

Austin came from the horse stable and confronted Wanda.

"My brother told me you're a witch and you put a spell on me to make me love you. Is this true?" asked Austin, feeling betrayed.

"It was the only way I could get you to notice me. Then I was afraid that, if the potion wore off, you wouldn't like me anymore," explained Wanda.

"I already noticed you before. I would look for you after the competitions were over, and you were never there. Now I don't want anything to do with you," Austin said, showing a little anger.

"Because I'm a witch?" asked Wanda, nearly sobbing.

"No. Because you used your magical powers on me," said Austin. "Now I can't trust you anymore. How would I really know if they're my true feelings or just some magical spell?" he turned away from Wanda and walked toward the barn where Marlin was working.

When she saw Marlin look at her, Wanda yelled, "On both of you, the moonlit curse will fall upon. Neither of you will ever sleep when the moon is full."

Crying, Wanda turned and disappeared in a whirlwind of flames.

At the next full moon cycle, far from town, Wanda had set up a witching circle out in a secluded area. First, she traced the circle with the tip of her broom in a counterclockwise motion. Then, slowly going clockwise, she filled the traced line with rock salt, closing her inside.

Inside the circle, Wanda stood by a small fire and tossed in wolf bane. "Luna Bright, bring you fright. Attack this one this night."

On the burning wolf bane, Wanda dropped a miniature effigy of Austin Hallmark.

That night, Austin dreamed that thirteen wolves had attacked him, ripped his flesh from his bones, and left him for dead. That next morning, Marlin found Austin in a blood-soaked bed. Bite marks with claw tears were all over Austin's body. Marlin washed his wounds and dressed them as Austin lay there in a coma.

That same afternoon, Marlin received an odd visitor. Winston Wisestone came and explained what Wanda had done the night before in her witching circle.

He said, "There is only one way to end this curse. You must shoot a silver-tipped arrow through your brother's heart when he turns into the werewolf under the full moon." Then Winston handed Marlin a mysterious-looking black bag. "This will help you in your quest to track down your brother between full moons."

Being only sixteen, Marlin couldn't fathom the idea of what this stranger had told him about werewolves, silver arrows, and killing his brother to save himself from the curse. Later in life, he understood all too well.

Winston Wisestone had been the mysterious man in Broomstick. He covertly mingled in affairs of the nonmagical population when they crossed over into the wizarding community. His unknown action was that of a sleuth wizard.

Winston stood six feet tall with a thin build. He kept his dark hair short and styled to the shape of his head. Except to his close wizard friends, he was a quiet sort. He never talked of his past before he came to Broomstick.

Winston loved Harriet, but he hadn't told her or even acknowledged her affection, fearing the people searching for him would find out where he was. Harriet, on the other hand, was very overt about how she felt toward Winston. At the Poison Apple, Harriet would come up behind Winston wrap her arms around him, and squeeze him.

"Hiya, Winston," she would always say.

Winston just sat there with his thoughts. Out of anguish, he mentally screamed at the top of his lungs.

Winston's problem started before he came to Broomstick. When he was born, his parents did what aristocratic families had always done. They signed a betrothal contract with another aristocratic family. When he turned sixteen, he quietly left home. Behind him, he covered his exit with charms and enchantments. When needed, he used strong double-edged spells as he hid his escape.

By the age of twenty, Winston had a good enchantment umbrella that kept him cloaked. He found his way to the town of Broomstick and hid himself among those who would least suspect a dark, gloomy background. He applied for a job at McDermit Broomstick, and he was hired to test-fly brooms.

Harriet saw Winston for the first time at the Poison Apple. Winston sat with other wizards who worked with him at the Broomstick factory. Harriet tried to get Winston's attention. With her hip, Harriet bumped into Winston's chair. Winston just politely smiled and turned back to the conversation. One time, Harriet grabbed a serving platter of toadstool soup and dropped it on Winston as if it were an accident. He got up, ignored Harriet completely, excused himself to the other wizards, and went home.

Winston came in to the Hidden Quiddity and bought enchantment supplies. Harriet tried to wait on him, but Winston waited around until Agnes wasn't busy and purchased his wares.

Winston's friends pointed out to him, "She is falling all over you."

They asked the obvious question, "What are you waiting for? Halloween?"

Winston finally did slip one day, and he let it be known to his wizard friends.

He said, "I find Harriet to be a very nice witch. As a matter of fact, I would be happy just to spend the rest of my life discovering her inner magical secrets of witchcraft."

That was it. The word was on the street faster than a fairy could blink her eyes. When Harriet heard this, she planned devious ways to get Winston to talk to her. But they all failed.

Winston tested a new flying broom. The straw was weaved in a different pattern, and the rope was made of rayon. The new weave splintered into a dried-out cat hairball, and the rayon rope unraveled in mid-flight. From fifty feet in the air, Winston fell as he held the broomstick close. There on the test field, Winston crash-landed on the ground, still clutching the broomstick in his hands.

When Harriet heard the tragic news and found out that Winston was in the magical ward of Broomstick Hospital, she went to see him. Winston lay there, unable to move. With tears in her eyes, Harriet wrapped her arms around Winston. All she thought of to say was, "Hiya, Winston."

In the years after that, Winston did warm up to Harriet. He would smile at her when she came into the tavern. Harriet was more determined than ever to get Winston to talk to her, but it was only more plans and more failed attempts.

At the Renaissance Faire, Harriet had a special vial of double-strength with pixie dust love potion in her left pocket. In her right pocket, she also had a vial of fruit juice. This was the first day of the Renaissance Faire, and Harriet was ready for when JayCee strolled by the booth. Harriet's luck wasn't in sync at that moment. Winston passed the booth first.

In a bad British accent, Harriet called out, "Elow, Govner! Come try some love potion."

Off to one side, Penelope giggled.

"Come on, gov. This is just for fun," Harriet said, prodding Winston with her very bad accent.

Winston walked over to the booth. He smiled at Harriet. "I know all about your pranks you have been pulling. No tricks this time."

Harriet stood there, dumbfounded. "You talked to me, Winston," she said. Her eyes had that innocent, bewildered look of amazement that hadn't been there since she was a child.

"Is this your love potion?" asked Winston.

He reached out for the vial Harriet had set on the counter. Harriet looked down at the double strength laced with pixie dust vial of love potion in horror. Harriet knocked it over and spilled out the potion.

"Oh, sorry," said Harriet.

She handed him another vial of the love potion that was normally watered down. Winston drank it down.

Before it had taken any effect, he said, "I love you, Harriet."

Winston walked away from the booth without looking back. Harriet was about to call out to him when JayCee came around a corner and headed in their direction.

Chapter Thirteen
The Renaissance Faire

If you haven't been to the Renaissance Faire, I encourage you to go. For added fun, dress up for the occasion. The period is during the reign of Queen Elizabeth I. You can talk to actors about what is going on during that time period. Shopkeepers get into their roles very well. Be careful of the added-on taxes when buying wares. According the shopkeepers, the queen taxes everything. From clothing to ale mugs, many different booths sell wares. Many food items are available, like olive oils, spices, and herbs. Entertainment is everywhere with singers, dancers, musicians, and comedians. The big show is the royal tournament of horses with jousting battles. For those of you who dress for the faire, there is fun to be had in mingling with others such as yourself, playing as if you are really in the Renaissance period. I, of course, go as myself. Welcome to the world of the Renaissance Faire.

That particular summer was almost upon them in Broomstick. The mail came with the yearly pamphlets of many different programs and events that kept young teens out of trouble. But that didn't happen in the case of JayCee Münter.

Harriet was a prankster, a mischievous witch. But she wasn't the run-of-the-mill prankster who pulled jokes just to pull jokes. Harriet always had a purpose in mind for the pranks she had done. Agnes sent the pamphlet to the Münters about the Renaissance Faire, and she had added a charm to the pamphlet. But Harriet added on to it as well. The Münters initially decided to ignore it.

Agnes' and Harriet's booth promoted the Hidden Quiddity potion shop. Harriet gave out watered-down free samples of her love potion. The effect only lasted for five minutes before it wore off. The joke was that the person realized that, after five minutes, he or she had made a fool of himself or herself with a stranger walking by. But things never go the right way when dealing with magical potions and love.

At the Münter household, the usual junk mail had filled their mailbox. With a teenager in the house, the program pamphlets had come in droves this first summer that JayCee was thirteen. There were marching band camps, a science fair, weight loss seminars, and sport leagues pamphlets from all over the country.

But one was different from the rest. Like the others, it was folded in three tiers. But, unlike the rest, it had been printed on old parchment, and the words were written in Old English-style lettering. On the front, it read, "The Renaissance Faire."

Since it had been charmed, it sat right on top of the mail. But Jay just tossed it off to the side to be shredded later. The next morning at the breakfast table, the pamphlet sat on top of his coffee. Folded open, it showed the free coupon.

"Cindy, did you set this here?" asked Jay.

"No. Maybe JayCee did," answered Cindy.

"Free for the entire month," said Jay, laughing. "I'm sure there is a catch to this."

He tore the pamphlet in half and threw it in the trash. Later that morning at work, the pamphlet again appeared in Jay's reports. Right on front of the double-charmed pamphlet was the words, "No catch."

"Someone has pulled a good prank here," thought Jay.

He stuck his head out of his office, looking at the cubicles of the accounting staff. "Very funny joke, whoever you are," said Jay, waving the pamphlet above his head.

Cindy found the pamphlet in the refrigerator, sitting next to the milk, also with the words "No catch" on the front.

"Strange," she thought. "Didn't Jay tear this up and put it in the trash?"

Cindy sat the pamphlet on her shredding pile for later and forgot about it.

During the finance meeting that afternoon with H.G. White, the pamphlet had been taped to one of the cardboard graphs. When Jay changed to a new chart, the charmed pamphlet once again appeared. This time, across the inside of the pamphlet, was big, bold Old English lettering that read, "This is not a joke."

Jay thought to himself, "This has gone too far."

Back in his office, another charmed pamphlet sat on top of the business mail on his desk.

"That's it!" said Jay.

With the three pamphlets in his hand, Jay walked to the copy/shredder room. Later in life, Jay admitted this had been the biggest mistake he had ever made with magical materials. He fed the pamphlets into the double crosscut shredder. Not long after, an office staff member knocked on his door.

"Excuse me, Mr. Münter, but the copy machine is making copies on funny-looking paper. It won't stop, even after I unplugged it."

Jay stood there and watched the copy machine continue to make copies of the pamphlet.

He said to the copy machine, "Okay, I'll look at the pamphlet."

The copy machine stopped printing.

"Shall I just shred the rest of these, Mr. Münter?" the staff person asked.

"No! Just box them up, please. I'll take them home," Jay said. His voice trembled a little.

About the same time that the copy machine had been stopped, Cindy started to shred papers and junk mail. The phone rang back in Cindy's office. She walked back and answered the phone.

Jay asked, "Did you find that Renaissance Faire pamphlet anywhere in the house?"

"Yes. In the refrigerator by the milk," answered Cindy. "I was about to shred it with the junk mail."

"Don't shred it!" roared Jay, forcing Cindy to pull the phone away from her ear.

School was out for the summer, and JayCee needed the break from studying. He pulled straight As, which made his parents very proud. Actually, JayCee studied very hard because it kept his mind off this peculiar sense that he must go somewhere and someone watched him day and night.

On the last day of school, pamphlets had been handed out with summer activities. One odd pamphlet only came in JayCee's packet. It was printed on old parchment-type paper. Printed on the front was "Renaissance Faire." JayCee opened the pamphlet and found a coupon that said, "Free admission for the whole month."

"I need to go to this," JayCee thought as he felt a different urge than usual.

That evening at dinner, JayCee asked, "Could I go to the Renaissance Faire? I have this free coupon for a monthlong pass from a pamphlet I received at school. There will be knights on horses, outdoor plays, and people dressed up like old times. It could be a good history lesson."

JayCee hadn't known of what happened to his parents that day. Both Jay and Cindy weren't surprised that JayCee had brought one home from school.

"Okay. You can go only if all your yard work is kept up," said Jay.

On the first day of the Renaissance faire, JayCee walked around, took in some of the shows, ate Ye Olde English food, and watched the people who were dressed in Renaissance clothing. JayCee had just turned down a curved row of booths when a woman called out to him.

Harriet had a hard decision to make when JayCee came around a corner and headed in their direction. She wanted to call out to Winston. Instead, she chose the intended target of their plan.

Harriet turned her head and yelled out in her bad English accent, "Hey now, lad! Come on over, and try our love potion."

"What will happen when I drink it?" asked JayCee, feeling a strange tingle behind his ears.

"You'll have girls falling in love with you," Harriet lied, still using her bad accent.

"I don't think I'll try it," said JayCee.

He began to walk away, uncertain about what he had felt. It was as if that woman had lied to him about how the love potion worked. Just at that moment, Penelope came out from behind the curtain in the back into the booth.

JayCee tried not to stare, but he used his peripheral vision instead. His heart had started to beat a little faster than normal. JayCee tried not to be obvious. He strolled down a couple of booths and then looked back at the girl. To JayCee, for some strange reason, this girl looked natural dressed in the Renaissance-era clothing, as if she came from that century. Then JayCee saw her magical green eyes.

JayCee felt that strange sensation behind his ears. It pounded against his eardrums, like words echoing from far away. They were too loud and too numerous to be coherent.

Harriet had seen JayCee looking back at Penelope.

"Come on. Come on back this way," she said to herself.

Harriet moved Penelope around the booth, like a worm on a baited hook.

"You know you want to meet her," Harriet talked to herself.

Another boy came up to the booth and asked Penelope, "What's your name?"

"Get lost, kid," Harriet said in a maternal, protective voice.

JayCee wandered back near the booth. He noticed that, the closer he got to the potions booth, the less his ears pounded with the echoed sound. He hoped the woman would call out again to try the love potion.

"If she was telling the truth about how the love potion worked, that wouldn't be fair to the girl," thought JayCee as he hesitated at the booth just before the potions booth.

"What if it wore off and she didn't like me?" JayCee thought to himself.

Harriet pulled him over to one side away from Penelope and whispered to JayCee, "There's no harm in trying it, and it won't last long. Only a minute or two. Then it is gone. It's just for fun, you know."

Harriet reached into her pockets. She tried to find the vial she had prepared for JayCee with just the fruit juice.

"Here you go," she said as she found the vial in one of the pockets. "Just drink it up."

Harriet moved JayCee in direct eyesight of Penelope as he drank down the vial. He choked a little on the oversweetened juice and dropped the vial on the ground.

Penelope didn't notice JayCee at first. Then she realized a boy was staring at her, and he wasn't blinking his eyes. Penelope wasn't able to move around the booth without JayCee moving his eyes in her direction. An uneasy feeling came over Penelope.

Agnes came in the booth and saw JayCee as he stood there with a glazed stare, looking toward Penelope.

"Hello, JayCee. We met before, although you may not remember me," Agnes said, trying to break his gaze from Penelope.

"I'm Agnes Candlewick. This is my sister Harriet. Over here is our cousin Penelope, who is visiting us from England. Penelope, this is JayCee Münter."

"Pleased to meet you, JayCee," Penelope said, bowing very ladylike.

"Say hello, JayCee, to Miss Penelope," Harriet rang in.

"H … Hello, Miss Penelope," said JayCee in a rough voice that was left from his choked cough.

Agnes picked up the vial that sat on the counter and smelled it.

"This is the double-strength potion you had for Winston, and it has pixie dust in it!" Agnes whispered strongly in Harriet's ear.

Harriet looked at the vial. "That is the one I knocked over from when Winston was here. I didn't give JayCee—"

Agnes interrupted Harriet. As usual, she had to take control of the situation. She knew this wasn't an easy fix.

"JayCee, why don't you come back here with us for a while?" suggested Agnes.

Penelope figured out that Harriet had given JayCee a vial of the love potion. She knew it wouldn't last long. After a few minutes, JayCee began to talk to Penelope.

JayCee asked Penelope questions about her, but he didn't comprehend the answers, as they were unusually different then he expected.

JayCee stumbled with his first question. "Um, what's it like in … um … where you're from?"

"Well, I haven't seen much outside of Dragonstep, but it is a wonderful magical valley secluded in the Border Forest between England and Scotland. Overlooking the valley is a castle that has a curse surrounding it," described Penelope.

"Do you have any brothers or sisters?" asked JayCee.

"No, I'm the only one so far. My parents say I'm there one and only bewitchery," stated Penelope, smiling and blushing.

"Your cousin said you're visiting for the summer. How did you decide to come here?" inquired JayCee, still staring intently at Penelope.

"My father suggested I should visit my uncle in Salem to see the outside world. I really didn't want to be watched over. So I found Agnes and Harriet on our family tree and wrote them to see if they would allow me to stay with them," said Penelope.

"What school subjects do you like the best? I like science the best," commented JayCee.

"I think my best subject was potions and charms. I didn't do well in magical metazoan or necromancy," said Penelope with a very serious expression.

Her answers were strange to JayCee, but, at that time, he didn't care. He loved her. Every so often, he would tell Penelope almost as if someone else said it.

Penelope got embarrassed, and her face turned bright red. Penelope knew it was the love potion Harriet had given him. Still, Penelope found it was hard not to turn red, especially when Harriet egged it on.

"Go on. Tell her again," Harriet prodded JayCee. "She likes to hear it."

Not long after, Penelope thought something had gone bad with the love potion, especially since Agnes was cautiously watching JayCee. About three hours went by before the effects wore off. JayCee realized it, and he was very embarrassed. He ran home, feeling like a big jerk.

The next day, JayCee did not go to the Renaissance Faire. He mowed the lawn, trimmed bushes, and pulled weeds out of the garden. He tried to stop thinking of Penelope, but he couldn't. Every time he thought about drinking that love potion, he would get upset with himself and kick something.

"Now this girl won't even talk to me because of how I acted," JayCee thought to himself as he stuffed the last of weeds into a bag.

JayCee also tried to ignore the echoed voices in his ears. It sometimes seemed that he understood the fragmented sounds. After he finished the yard work, he hid himself upstairs in his bedroom. He lay there on his bed with a pillow over his head.

In the afternoon, Cindy was in the kitchen, preparing to make dinner, when the doorbell rang. When she answered the door, a pretty, young girl with shoulder-length auburn hair and mysterious green eyes stood on the front porch. She was in a Renaissance Faire outfit. Cindy thought it was strange that she hadn't seen anyone walk up to the house from the kitchen.

"Excuse me, does JayCee Münter live here?" asked Penelope in an English accent that caught Cindy quite by surprise.

"My, you're such a lovely young girl. Did you meet JayCee yesterday at the Renaissance Faire?" asked Cindy, wondering if this English accent was all an act.

JayCee heard Penelope's voice and wondered why she was at the door. JayCee came downstairs from his bedroom and heard what Penelope had said to his mom.

"Thank you, milady." Penelope said, bowing gracefully. "My name is Penelope Candlewick. I came to apologize to JayCee for yesterday and for what my Cousin Harriet had done."

Penelope noticed that JayCee stood back away from the door. She intentionally spoke to JayCee indirectly, right through Cindy. Cindy gave the girl a puzzled look.

"Apologize for what?" asked Cindy, looking back at JayCee for an answer.

JayCee jumped into the conversation and tried to circumvent the answer as to what took place the day before at the potions booth.

"I am the one who needs to apologize to you," said JayCee, stepping closer to the door.

"It was a misunderstanding, Mom," JayCee answered. He used a boyish expression and hoped that would stop the inquisition.

Cindy eyed both JayCee and this girl with suspicion. Then she left them alone and went back to work in the kitchen. She kept her ear tuned in to what they said next. JayCee invited Penelope into the living room, a large room with an open ceiling and large, stone fireplace. It was just a step down from the entrance into the house.

JayCee directed Penelope over to a high-back couch with old-style wooden arms. Penelope sat down at one end while JayCee sat at the other end, facing at an angle toward Penelope.

"So what you were telling me about where you live and what school subjects you like, you were just joking around with me, right?" asked JayCee, hoping for a plausible answer.

"No, it is actually the truth. I was honestly answering your questions. I was trying to be sincere with you." She leaned toward JayCee and whispered, "There is more I need to tell you, but not here. Your mother is listening, and it could be embarrassing to explain." She then raised her voice. "Would you like to go the Renaissance Faire?" Her voice then returned to a whisper. "My cousins want to talk to you about something very important."

"I'm not going near your cousins. They made me act foolish and feel like a dumb jerk in front of you. It was stupid of me to drink that love potion just to meet you. I knew better," whispered JayCee. "Your cousins shouldn't be giving stuff like that to kids. It was wrong." JayCee felt a little angry. The echoing voices vibrated deep inside. "But I would like to go the faire with you though," continued JayCee, calming down.

"We will talk on the way to the faire then," said Penelope, staring at JayCee with her emerald eyes.

JayCee called out to his mom, "I'll be at the faire, Mom. I'll be back in time for dinner."

Acting like she hadn't listened to them talk, Cindy answered back, "Okay, kids, have fun. If you like, Penelope can come for dinner also."

But Cindy was really hoping to find out who this unusual strange girl was and what the secrecy was all about.

JayCee and Penelope were out the front door before they could give an answer.

They walked slowly to the street. Cindy peered out the window. She watched JayCee and this mysterious, spooky young girl as they walked away.

Penelope stopped and turned to JayCee after they were out of hearing distance of Cindy. "I am a witch. My father is a wizard, and my mother is a witch. "My two cousins are witches as well."

This did not surprise JayCee. He somehow felt like it was familiar to him, as if it were normal.

"You got my cousins all wrong. Harriet did not give you any love potion at all. That double-strength love potion was for a wizard friend. Harriet wanted to get him to notice her, but she changed her mind and purposefully spilled it. Cousin Harriet gave you a vial filled with fruit juice," explained Penelope. "Cousin Agnes knows about your magical powers. Agnes thinks they control your emotions. So, when you drank the fruit juice and thought it was a love potion, your magical power gave you a blast of self-induced love potion. I was upset that Harriet would even think of doing something like that to a really nice boy that I wanted to meet."

"That's when Agnes told me that Harriet didn't give you any potion at all and you have magical powers. This is what they need to talk to you about. You were showing your true emotions, but your own magic was enhancing them. I know you do not really love me as we just met. But I still want to start a friendship with you."

When Penelope finished talking and noticed the expression on JayCee's face, she thought, "I've gone too far."

JayCee's face had gone from embarrassment red to flush pale. The sickened feeling that he had felt the day before had come back. As they walked down the street, JayCee grabbed hold of Penelope's hand. The echoing sounds in JayCee ears subsided. JayCee felt like the voices had left him.

Penelope realized instantly what had just happened, but she said nothing because she felt a strange sensation of being happy to be with JayCee as they held hands.

Cindy kept watching her son and the mystery girl through the kitchen window. When JayCee reached out and held Penelope's hand, Cindy observed a glowing aura of colors surrounding the two of them. Trouble was the word that was imprinted on Cindy's mind.

Chapter Fourteen
The Tests

Agnes and Harriet were at their booth. Harriet handed out a sample of her love potion to another unwitting victim of her prank when Penelope and JayCee walked up. Agnes noticed that JayCee and Penelope were holding hands. Something was different about the expression on Penelope's face. It was in her eyes. The way she looked at JayCee, Agnes felt an aura of déjà vu within herself.

Harriet spoke first when JayCee stood with Penelope at the front of the booth. Apologetically, she said, "JayCee, I'm really not a bad witch. I may be mischievous now and then."

"Is it true that you only gave me fruit juice?" asked JayCee, grasping for assurance of what Penelope had said.

"Cross my fingers and not to spell," said Harriet. "And I would like for us to be friends, too."

Agnes interrupted and began to talk before Harriet said anything that would have jeopardized their second chance with JayCee. "I want to help you understand your magical power, JayCee. I need you to take a few tests to find out what your abilities are. I also need to know where your magical power came from.

After the faire is over, we can spend more time together." She looked for a sign that JayCee had begun to warm up to them.

JayCee didn't say much. He had the strangest feeling come over him that this was the right place to be and Agnes was to be a very good friend to him.

JayCee and Penelope spent the rest of the time together while the faire was open. The faire was in a park beside a lake. As the sun shone through the tall trees, they made freakish shadows that moved with the breeze. Under some trees sat fairies to entertain children with games.

Penelope would smile at the fairies and wink as if she knew a secret about them. People at booths with high-flying flags of the century gone by called out to visitors to come and take a look at their wares. JayCee and Penelope explored booths, watched plays, and talked about the magical world Penelope lived in. JayCee was finding out so much about Penelope and the magical world that he was being drawn into.

Every day, JayCee met Penelope at the potions booth, or she would suddenly show up at his door as he was leaving.

When they met, Penelope made sure they held hands. It wasn't just the pixie dust that gave her happiness. Something was there that Penelope just couldn't quite figure out. It made her so happy when she was with JayCee.

Of course, when the two of them held hands, JayCee felt this happy sensation all over him. But, at the time, JayCee didn't know about the pixie dust.

On one of those days, JayCee and Penelope walked through a creepy-looking candle booth with gargoyle candleholders, skulls with wax melted down the face, and scented oils for purification spells.

JayCee suddenly asked, "What is it like to live in a world of magic?"

"I don't know. I guess it would be like how I'm seeing your world without it," said Penelope.

"Tell me more about your school," asked JayCee.

Penelope described the courses she had taken. JayCee interrupted occasionally with "What does this mean?" or "What does that mean?"

"This one class teaches us how to distinguish between a spell and an enchantment, compared to a charm," explained Penelope, like JayCee knew what she was talking about.

"Wait? A spell? To me, that is what you do with words," said JayCee.

"Exactly," said Penelope.

JayCee asked, "Exactly what?"

"To do a spell, it is done with words," stated Penelope.

"So, if I want to have something, I spell it?" asked JayCee, trying to understand.

"Well, that is more of materialization than a spell," explained Penelope.

"So what am I doing when I'm spelling?" JayCee continued.

"You make things happen," Penelope said.

"All right, let me see if this works. M-A-K-E I-T R-A-I-N," said JayCee, spelling it out.

"What are you doing?" asked Penelope.

"I was spelling 'make it rain,'" said JayCee.

Penelope laughed. "Is that what they teach you at your school about witchcraft?"

"They don't teach anything about witchcraft at all," said JayCee.

She gave JayCee a perplexed look. "A spell is a chant. But you eventually work it down to an action word. And, when you're really good, you just think it and point your wand. Some witches can use just their two fingers, like Agnes and Harriet."

"Could you teach me a spell?" asked JayCee.

"I'll show you two spells. One with a chant and one with an action word," said Penelope. "Be da lee de da lee bunkins boos. Make JayCee's strings untie his shoes."

JayCee watched in amazement as his shoes untied themselves. "This is real magic," he thought.

Penelope pointed her wand at JayCee's shoestrings. "Stringara."

JayCee's shoes were retied.

JayCee asked, "Can I try to do that spell with your magic wand?"

"Wands don't work that way. Your wand is chosen for you," explained Penelope.

JayCee had an idea. He pointed the fingers on his right hand down the row of booths. and said, "Stringara."

People fell over, and shoes went flying in all directions.

Penelope pushed JayCee away from the catastrophe that occurred.

"Let's quickly go to another part of the faire," she instructed.

Penelope and JayCee ducked into a gypsy fortune-teller's booth to hide while the crowd settled down. Madam Olga was in the middle of telling the future of a customer with tarot cards when her trance was interrupted. She dropped the cards on the floor. The only card that was turned upward was the Judgment card.

The Judgment card was often a hard card to read. It usually signaled a big change that involved leaving something old completely behind to step into something completely new. It also partially dealt with very hard and final decisions. It meant facing something that most don't want to face.

"You can't hide any longer. All the dead have risen and are out in the open. Face what you have to face. Make that decision. Change," said Madam Olga with a disturbed expression.

She stared intently at the two youngsters who barged into her canvas tent. JayCee and Penelope backed out without saying a word.

Each day, JayCee asked more about the magical world. It enthused him so much. Penelope talked about elves and nymphs like they were ordinary creatures. She did say that pixies were special and she had a pixie of her own. Then Penelope realized she needed to tell JayCee about Sunshine and her special pixie dust.

"My pixie's name is Sunshine. Every day, she gives me pixie dust to rub into my hands," explained Penelope. "I'm sorry I didn't tell you this before, but the pixie dust makes people feel happy. When we hold hands, you get the pixie dust also. It may cause you to be happy to be with me. If you don't want to hold my hand anymore, I'll understand. I guess I should also tell you I have a fire-breathing dragon for a pet."

"You have a fire-breathing dragon for a pet?" exclaimed JayCee.

Near the last days of the Renaissance Faire, JayCee told Penelope of the paper bag trick he did when he was seven years old and how it angered his dad. On the last day of the faire, JayCee told Penelope a secret, something he had never shared with anyone else.

"I keep having this dream about a man with long, brown hair and a long beard fighting for his life. He keeps saying, 'I will not let you!'"

"You must tell this to Agnes, JayCee. A wizard friend of Cousin Agnes has been missing for thirteen years, and he fits that description," insisted Penelope as she stood in front of JayCee and held both of his hands. "I know you told me in confidence. I really like that you trust me with your secret, but this may help them."

JayCee sat at dinner with his parents and talked about the last day of the faire. "The closing parade was as good as the opening one," said JayCee.

Cindy asked, "How are you and Penelope getting along?"

"We're having a great time, but I'm not sure what we are going to do now the Renaissance Faire is over," said JayCee. "Um, I've been asked if I could go out to dinner with Penelope and her cousins this week."

Jay said, "We need to meet Penelope's cousins, and I still haven't met Penelope either. How about asking them to dinner here first?"

"Okay, I'll ask them tomorrow," said JayCee.

Early the next morning, Penelope appeared on the front porch at JayCee's house. Cindy answered the door and invited Penelope into the kitchen. JayCee wasn't out of bed yet. Cindy tried to have little chats when Penelope showed up at the door on the days that JayCee didn't meet Penelope at the potions booth. But this day was different because the faire was over.

"Well, what are you and JayCee going to do today?" asked Cindy.

"We have been at the faire so much that I haven't really seen the town. After all, I came here to see Broomstick, not to play Old England," said Penelope, giggling.

"JayCee told us last night that you and your cousins would like to take JayCee out for dinner this week," stated Cindy. "However, we would like to meet your cousins first."

"Oh, they would love to meet you also," said Penelope. "They have been so busy at the faire and couldn't make time to come over."

"What is your cousin's phone number?" asked Cindy. "I'll call her and see if they can come to dinner tonight."

Penelope almost asked what a phone number was when JayCee came into the kitchen.

Seeing the puzzled look on Penelope's face, JayCee said, "I can have Agnes give you a call, Mom. I'm sure her and Harriet are busy trying to get their novelty shop back in order to open up today."

"I can ask them also," said Penelope. "Thank you very kindly for the invitation."

JayCee and Penelope went out the kitchen door before any other conversation could have started.

"I was going to ask Agnes about dinner because my dad wants to meet your cousins before he will let me go out to dinner with all of you," explained JayCee. "So how far is your cousin's potion shop from here?"

Penelope pulled JayCee over near a large tree that was just off to the side of the house.

"Hold both my hands," said Penelope. "Close your eyes."

A warming air circled both of them and then stopped just as quickly as it came.

"You can open your eyes now," said Penelope.

JayCee looked around and saw they were standing outside a shop with a sign that read, "The Hidden Quiddity."

"This is Agnes' and Harriet's potion shop," said Penelope.

She opened the door and led JayCee inside. JayCee looked around and saw bottles of dry ingredients and colored liquids, black pots, and other strange things. JayCee was in wonderment of what and how this had to do with magic. He wanted to ask a thousand questions. He was tempted to pick up stuff for a closer look until a potted plant wrapped a vine around his wrist and moved his hand away.

Agnes was behind the counter, and Harriet was stacking a new shipment of brooms.

Penelope walked up to the counter. "JayCee's parents would like to meet you, and they have invited us to dinner tonight."

JayCee stood there bewildered for a moment and then turned toward Agnes with his hands in his pockets.

"My dad wants to meet you before he will allow me to stay out for dinner," explained JayCee. "And my mom wants you to call her."

"I want to meet your parents also," said Agnes. "I have some questions for them as well."

"We'll come to dinner tonight," stated Agnes.

Agnes looked away from JayCee and Penelope. "Mrs. Münter?" There was a short pause before Agnes spoke again. "This is Agnes Candlewick. Along with Penelope, my sister and I would love to come to dinner tonight." Agnes paused again. "Six o'clock is just fine." Agnes smiled politely at JayCee. "Thank you for the invitation. Good-bye."

Looking perplexed, JayCee asked, "How did you do that? Can you teach me that trick?"

Agnes replied, "I don't do tricks. I do magical things. Now that you are here, I would like to start on the tests we talked about."

Agnes escorted JayCee to the back of the store. She sat JayCee down at the round table where the blackened crystal ball sat undisturbed. She placed a glass plate in front of him.

"Hold your right hand over the plate and see if you can make it rise," she instructed.

JayCee held his right hand over the plate. "Do I say anything?"

"No, just concentrate on the plate," said Agnes.

JayCee stared at the plate. Suddenly, the plate shot away and smashed against the wall.

Agnes replaced the plate. "Now try it with your left hand."

JayCee held his left hand over the plate. It shook and rattled on the table. Then the plate slowly rose up to JayCee's left hand.

Agnes took the plate away. "You can relax now."

"Does that mean anything?" asked JayCee.

"So far, it means you can levitate plates," joked Harriet.

"Hold these two clear crystals, one in each hand. And squeeze," said Agnes.

White smoke rolled out of his left hand while black smoke came from his right hand.

"Open your hands, JayCee," said Agnes.

The crystal in JayCee's right hand was white, but the crystal in his left hand was black. Harriet gasped, and Penelope stared in bewilderment.

"One more test, JayCee," said Agnes, concerned with the results of the crystal test. "Stand over here in front of the scrying mirror. Extend your arms forward. With your index and middle fingers, point at yourself. Now cross your fingers on your left hand."

Penelope appeared in the mirror in place of his reflection. A shadowed person stood behind her.

"Now uncross your fingers and cross your fingers on your right hand," said Agnes.

JayCee uncrossed his left fingers and then crossed his two right fingers. The air in the room chilled. It was like being at a dead man's party. The mirror had an eerie glow within the reflection. Two wizards were gripping each other in a battle of strength. One wizard was in a black robe, and the other was wearing a gray cloak.

Harriet said it first, "McDermit, Agnes! It's McDermit!"

JayCee uncrossed his fingers and collapsed on the floor. Penelope ran over to JayCee. But Agnes was there first. She helped JayCee up off the floor and into a chair.

Agnes said to Penelope, "Rub your hands with pixie dust. Then rub his forehead and neck."

Sunshine had come out from behind Penelope's left ear, where she was sleeping, and dusted Penelope's hands. Penelope rubbed her hands together. As Penelope massaged JayCee's forehead and neck with the pixie dust, she contemplated the images that were in the mirror.

"What did it mean when he crossed his left fingers and I appeared in the mirror?" questioned Penelope. "And who was that shadowy figure behind me?"

"It's complicated for you because you're only thirteen years old. But you have given JayCee the key to control the source of his magical power. Before the two of you met, I suspect the source of his magical power haunted him in his dreams and possibly even while he was awake to do something or retrieve and bring something to a place unknown to him," explained Agnes.

Agnes revealed the real problem that had haunted JayCee since birth and what had happened to Franklin McDermit.

"JayCee has a wizard within him, or at least his magical powers. He also seems to have the magical powers of Franklin McDermit," said Agnes. She peered over toward the still-blackened crystal ball. "Wherever that one wizard is, that is where we will find Franklin. The unknown wizard's power is black magic. Apparently, the older JayCee is, the stronger the black magic is becoming."

Agnes spoke directly to Penelope on this point. "Now you have given him the one thing he needed to control this black magical source and resists its temptations. Harriet saw it in your tea leaves when you first arrived.

"What I read in your tea leaves that day is that you were going to become a boy's one true love," said Harriet.

"I used that information to my advantage by getting JayCee to meet us through you. We needed him to help find out what happened to Franklin. I didn't know this was the kind of trouble I got you mixed up in," continued Harriet. "I thought about giving JayCee that double-strength potion I had made for Winston to ensure he would fall in love with you. I couldn't even bring myself to do such a terrible thing like that to Winston. I knocked it over on purpose to keep Winston from drinking it. JayCee fell in love with you on his own and without any help from me."

Agnes tried to explain what all this meant to Penelope, but even she had a hard time understanding this whole situation. "You are JayCee's one true love. Because of that, he has the power to control this black magic. For any reason you cause him grief and a broken heart, he will fall to the black side forever. This is not a burden to take lightly. As a young girl, I know it will be difficult for you to comprehend," stated Agnes.

"How do I know if he is my one true love?" asked Penelope. A tear was forming in one eye.

"I can't answer that," said Agnes sadly. "Only time and maturity will tell you."

"Then, for right now, I will be his true love, and he will be mine," stated Penelope. She leaned over and kissed JayCee on the cheek while she still rubbed his forehead with pixie dust.

Harriet asked, "What about McDermit and that other wizard? How can that be the source of JayCee's magical power? And what makes it black magic?"

"Not exactly all black magic," stated Agnes. "The crystals show that two forces are working here. One is protecting JayCee from the other, but he was slowly losing until Penelope's powerful magic of love tipped the power struggle. Now we must find where Franklin is if we want to help save both JayCee and him," said Agnes.

"JayCee is coming around," said Penelope.

"How are you feeling, JayCee?" asked Agnes.

"My head is spinning, and I feel like someone socked me in the stomach. But I feel happy to be here," said JayCee.

His eyes rolled around, unsure of what direction they should have looked. His facial expression showed he had a little too much pixie dust. Harriet saw it coming first. She went to the front of the shop and grabbed for a small cauldron. JayCee let go of what little he ate for breakfast. The smell of sour milk with soggy cereal encircled his head and made him more nauseated. After JayCee calmed down from the pixie dust, Agnes closed up shop for lunch, and the four of them went over to the Poison Apple.

As he walked into the tavern, JayCee noticed a strange sensation of déjà vu come over him.

"I've been here before. But that's not possible," JayCee said, puzzled.

JayCee also noticed that Penelope was holding onto his arm tightly. They sat down in a booth in the back corner.

An old witch came over to the table. "Hello, Agnes. Hello, Harriet."

JayCee spoke out of turn, "Hello, Bee, I'll have the usual tall ale and finger niblets."

"Now, who are you, young man?" asked the old witch.

JayCee crouched down. "I'm sorry. I don't know why I said that."

Bee turned to Agnes and Harriet. "He said that just like ol' McDermit used to." Then Bee turned to JayCee. "Whatcha gone and done, McDermit? Used too much de-aging potion? Is that why you haven't been around?"

Agnes stepped in. "This is JayCee Münter, Bee. We think he may be related."

"Now how about our lunch order," said Agnes, changing the subject. "Four rich, foamy, carbonated witch hazelnut sodas and a dragon patty with swamms, cheese curds, and slug sausage."

While Agnes talked to Bee, Penelope whispered in JayCee's ear, "Please tell them about your dreams."

JayCee whispered back, "For you, I will."

Penelope still held onto JayCee's arm and gave him a tight squeeze. JayCee wondered what made Penelope change so she had begun to show affection toward him. Before the tests, they were just good friends. JayCee didn't dwell on this change too long. He actually liked it.

"I need to tell you about a dream I have had over the years," said JayCee. "It's about the man in the mirror with long, brown hair and a beard wearing the gray cloak. In my dreams, he's fighting for his life and saying, 'I will not let you.' Is that Franklin McDermit? What did those tests tell you about me and him?" asked JayCee, worrying what the answers might bring for his future.

"It seems that your birth and Franklin McDermit's disappearance are connected in some way. Your magical power came to you after you were born, which means that, whatever McDermit was up to, he needed you," stated Agnes. "We think the other wizard in the mirror may be ..." Agnes looked toward Penelope. "Your father's reference to an ancient sorcerer called Oozar, which, for some reason, needs you, JayCee, as well. Because of this, you have both white and black magical powers within you."

JayCee remembered Penelope's image was in the mirror also. "What about Penelope's image in the mirror when I crossed my left finger?"

"Oh, this is getting good," said Harriet with a bewitched expression on her face. "Can I tell him?"

"Be nice, and be honest," said Agnes.

"Once upon a time long ago, there was a boy who met a girl who was a witch. He was spellbound with her, and she enchanted him with pixie dust. The boy couldn't help himself. He fell madly in love with the little witch girl," said Harriet.

"Stop it," said Agnes. "Because of your magical power, JayCee, you made yourself be attached to Penelope by falling in love with her at first sight. That love is helping you and McDermit control the black magic side. Penelope will always be your one true love. It is difficult for you to understand at you age. For right now, the two of you are just best friends, and you should look at it that way."

"Am I a wizard?" asked JayCee.

"Not exactly, said Agnes. "You're more of a ..." She paused. She didn't want to say, "pawn in a wizard's war." "Wizard apprentice to Franklin McDermit," she finally said.

When their food and drink came, Agnes and Harriet couldn't help but notice that people were whispering and pointing over their way.

JayCee looked at the dragon patty. "It's a pizza."

Harriet asked, "A what?"

JayCee said, "Oh, it's just another name for it."

And he left it at that.

Chapter Fifteen
Dinner at the Münters

Penelope and JayCee had to get back to JayCee's house to help his mom prepare for that night's dinner. Again, Penelope held JayCee's hands, and JayCee closed his eyes. The warming air came and went. JayCee and Penelope stood by the large tree, where they had started the morning.

"Do you believe what your cousins are saying about you and I?" asked JayCee.

He felt more comfortable with Penelope when they were alone to discuss that day's event.

"I don't think they would say anything like that if it wasn't true. For right now, I like you being my best friend," said Penelope.

She wrapped her arms around JayCee, gave him a loving hug, and placed her head on his shoulder. Cindy had just started to prepare dinner when she looked out the kitchen window and observed the hug Penelope gave JayCee. The two of them came in through the kitchen door, happy and smiling at each other.

"Well, it looks like the two of you must have had a nice day together," said Cindy.

JayCee didn't know what to say because of the strange events that had happened to him, so he brought up the subject of dinner.

"Agnes and Harriet will be here at six, and they are looking forward to meeting you and Dad," said JayCee, concerned about what he knew about Agnes and Harriet.

"Good. How about the two of you wash your hands and help me make dinner," said Cindy as she considered the next subject of conversation.

"I'd love to help. But I don't know how," said Penelope. "I'm not much of a kitchen witch."

Cindy stared at Penelope. "A what?"

Cindy was taken aback for a moment, thinking of when they first met. She thought of how Penelope's eyes could have bewitched someone with the spellbound stare she gave JayCee.

JayCee quickly started washing the fresh-picked vegetables in the sink. He hid his face from his mom as he just gasped for air.

"I'm sorry," said Penelope. "It's an old-world term for someone who specializes in cooking with all fresh ingredients."

Cindy got Penelope started on mixing dry ingredients for biscuit dough by following a recipe in a cookbook while she seasoned and wrapped a roast in aluminum foil to go into the oven. Penelope felt relaxed with this task, as it reminded her of mixing a potion in cauldron.

"If you please, Mrs. Münter, my cousins and I are allergic to bay leaves," stated Penelope before Cindy had a chance to season the roast.

"So, JayCee, have you learned about the difference in customs between the British and Americans?" asked Cindy, trying to jump-start a conversation.

"That's what we talked about a lot this past month," stated JayCee, unsure what led to this subject.

"Penelope, what does it mean in England when a girl hugs a boy?" asked Cindy, a little sheepish.

Penelope was bright on her toes and quickly came back with, "After you know someone a while, it is a nice way to say thank you to a friend."

"And what were you thanking JayCee for?" asked Cindy.

"Now," JayCee thought, "she is acting like a mother."

"Mom, please," said JayCee.

"I was thanking him for a wonderful day, Mrs. Münter. That's all," said Penelope. She knew that JayCee knew it meant more than that, and that pleased her.

"Okay, JayCee. I'm sorry," Cindy said, going on to a different subject. "I traveled to England years ago when I was in college. Where about are you from?"

"I come from a small town called Dragonstep. It's on the border between England and Scotland. It's in the Border Forest. From the air, they say the valley looks like a large dragon talon print," answered Penelope.

"A dragon's footprint the size of a valley," Cindy said, chuckling.

"That can't be true, of course. Everyone knows dragons do not grow that large," Penelope said, laughing a little. She hadn't thought much about what she had said.

JayCee looked nervous and laughed. "She has been making me laugh all month with her British humor."

Penelope thought, "I have to watch closely what I say tonight."

Jay drove home from work, feeling a little tired. He spent most of the afternoon in front of a computer screen. He put some drops into his eyes prior to leaving the office.

Just behind him in the driveway, Agnes and Harriet appeared. As they walked up the walkway to the front door, Jay looked in the rearview mirror just then. Jay did not believe it. He dismissed it and blamed his tired eyes.

Jay stepped out of the car. "Hello, you must be Agnes and Harriet Candlewick. I am Jay Münter, JayCee's father."

"I'm Agnes, and she's Harriet."

Agnes gestured toward her sister with her hand and then put out her hand for Jay's handshake. Jay opened the front door, gesturing to invite the two sisters in.

"Isn't your cousin from England coming tonight?" asked Jay.

"Penelope should already be here with JayCee," said Harriet.

Penelope and JayCee had set the table in the dining room while Cindy finished up in the kitchen. Cindy had just pulled out the roast from the oven and slid in the tray of biscuits when Jay opened the front door.

Jay escorted Agnes and Harriet into the living room. "Please, have a seat and relax. You two must be tired from your long walk."

Harriet started to say something, but Agnes punched in with, "Our friend let us off a little bit down the road so we could get in a short walk before dinner."

Cindy came in from the kitchen, holding a tray of glasses filled with a fruity, frothy drink.

"Welcome to our home," said Cindy.

"This is my wife, Cindy. This is Agnes and her sister Harriet," introduced Jay.

JayCee and Penelope came out from the dining room just as the oven buzzer in the kitchen went off.

"The biscuits are done," said Cindy. "Let's go into the dining room. I'll bring out dinner."

JayCee, Penelope, and Cindy went into the kitchen. As Cindy was taking the biscuits out of the oven, the tray slipped from Cindy's grip, even as she was holding onto a hot pad. Penelope reacted instinctively and kept the tray of biscuits from falling. She allowed Cindy to keep a hold of the tray and set it down on the counter.

Cindy looked at the tray, puzzled. She stood there and wondered how she managed to get them up on the counter without dropping the tray.

"That was a close one," stated Penelope.

The food was brought into the dining room without any further incident.

Conversation through dinner was light. It was mostly about the Renaissance Faire. One question was on Cindy's mind though.

"When Penelope first came to the house after the first day of the faire, she mentioned a misunderstanding and an apology," asked Cindy.

Before Agnes had a chance to try to stop her, Harriet spoke up quickly, "That was my fault. At our booth, we get into the Renaissance role-playing with the visitors at the faire. One of the fun things we do is give out a sample of love potion as a gag. I played with JayCee's young emotions a little too much when I was trying to get him to meet Penelope. I saw him coming by the booth and thought he looked like a nice boy. Being about the same age as Penelope, I played matchmaker by using Penelope's pretty looks and her interesting accent. I kind of made him look foolish in front of Penelope."

After dinner, everyone went into the living room once more. Agnes talked about the novelty shop. Jay kept his work talk low-key as to not bore anyone.

Eventually, Jay put something together in his mind. He said, "I knew a judge in college who taught financial law. His last name was Candlewick."

"That was our grandfather, Judge Benjamin Candlewick," announced Agnes. "He passed away just before I opened my store."

"He was your grandfather?" exclaimed Jay as he remembered some strange facts about Judge Candlewick. "That man knew things that even surprised the other professors. Some even said he dabbled in mysticism."

Agnes faked a laugh a little and changed the subject.

"Did you know Franklin McDermit?" asked Agnes.

"Isn't that the person who owned the broom company before Whitewing bought them out?" suggested Jay.

"You never met him then?" asked Agnes.

"No. He had been gone for a couple years before I was hired as an accountant," answered Jay.

The evening finally came to an end. This was where things almost became a disaster

Jay offered, "Could I give you a ride home since you didn't come in a car?"

Agnes said politely, "Our friend is coming to pick us up."

When the three of them walked outside, two bright lights came on at the end of the driveway. Agnes, Harriet, and Penelope walked toward the lights and disappeared.

The headlights pulled out of the drive way. To the Münters, it appeared a car had driven off into the darkness.

Chapter Sixteen
The Hidden Quiddity Potion Shop

Whenever Agnes needed advice, she visited her grandfather. Agnes remembered the day she went to see her grandfather to ask if she should open the potion shop.

In the late afternoon that day, Agnes traveled by broomstick to her grandpa's straw farm just outside of Broomstick. It was the day before the autumn equinox celebration. When Agnes landed her broomstick in the front yard, she saw Benjamin Candlewick sitting in his rocking chair on the porch. But he wasn't rocking back and forth.

Agnes walked up to the house quietly because she thought he was asleep. Agnes took one step at a time up to the porch. One of the steps creaked as Agnes stepped down on it.

Once up on the porch, Agnes found Grandpa Candlewick just sitting there quietly. A note lay in his lap, along with his ruby amulet and magic wand. Agnes sat down in the rocker next to him, the one her grandma used to rock in. She rocked with him for a while before she notified her parents and her sister.

The note said, "My amulet and magic wand is all that is left of the wizard within me. Use them to do something great, my little Agnes."

Benjamin Candlewick had lived to be one hundred and five years old.

Without the direct advice from her grandfather, Agnes went ahead with her plan and opened the potion shop. The name for the shop came from a story he had told her and Harriet when they were very young. His story started with, "The best things in life are always hidden from us, and they are never solid or concrete."

From that story, Agnes came up with the name of her potion shop, the Hidden Quiddity, in remembrance of Grandpa Candlewick.

Not long after she'd opened the Hidden Quiddity, a man had come in. He wore a business suit with a white shirt and tie. The suit, however, was soiled. From the shoulder down, he had a torn left sleeve. His shirt was stained with dried blood, and his tie was loosely tied around his neck. In his hands was an old oil lamp.

"This is a magical shop?" the man asked with a raspy voice.

As she looked at the unkempt, blood-stained man, she replied, "We're a novelty shop that carries magical equipment."

"I have here a special lamp that must be kept away from people like me. All I am asking for is your help. Can you use your magic to fix the trouble I am in?" pleaded the man as he sat down the old oil lamp on the counter in front of Agnes.

Agnes hesitated for a moment. At the time, she wondered if the man was pulling a trick on her. Agnes wasn't about to tell just anyone that wondered off the street that she was a witch. Agnes peered deep into the man's eyes. She felt in her bones his plight was genuine.

"That depends on what kind of trouble it is. Let's start with the lamp," noted Agnes.

She took out her wand and tapped on the lamp three times. Nothing happened.

"You have to rub the lamp to get him to come out," said the man.

Agnes stared right in the man's eyes. "That's how one gets into trouble with this lamp."

She tapped it again three times with her magic wand and said with an affirmative voice, "You come out of there now, or I'll dip this lamp into boiling hot, saltwater where no one will ever be able to rub it again and let you out."

Slowly, blue smoke rose out of the spout where a wick should be for an oil lamp. The blue smoke circled round and round until a figure from the waist up formed. The figure was wearing a turban and a velvety blue robe.

The genie looked at Agnes and then over to the man in soiled, bloody clothing.

"All I did was grant him what he asked for, no more and no less," said the genie to Agnes in his own defense.

"You!" said Agnes. "I thought the story was a fable to scare little witches and wizards from doing black magic."

"Who is he?" asked the man.

"Mister," said Agnes. "You have been duped by the one and only wizard who had a con game backfire in his face."

"He made a deal with the original genie of the lamp to help him gain control of a kingdom," explained Agnes.

"Through the power of black magic and the magic lamp, the wizard was to materialize from the lamp to gain access to the king's celebration. But the genie had a plan of his own and tricked the wizard into a scheme that freed the original genie from the lamp, leaving the wizard hidden inside." Agnes continued, "But the wizard became trapped, unable to escape the power of the lamp. There was a piece of the story that never changed because this was the terrifying part to little witches and wizards. The trapped wizard genie had an unmistakable mark on his left cheek. The original genie placed the tattoo on the wizard as a warning to the king. It was the pirate's skull and crossbones. We use it to mark poisons."

"Did you use all three wishes?" asked Agnes.

Looking terrified, the man said, "I have one more wish, but I would not use it because of how much trouble the other two wishes have caused."

"Well then, with my magical help and your last wish, we should be able to fix this mess, and I get to keep this lamp for safekeeping," stated Agnes, gazing directly into the eyes of the genie. "You will wish for the other two wishes to be rescinded and for your life to be restored back to the way it was before you wished for anything. Now, for you, genie, you will grant this man's last wish as intended and not as you want to interpret it. If you don't clear up the mess that you have caused in this man's life, I will free you from the lamp and personally preside over a Witch's Council as your judge. Are we clear on this, genie?"

"Crystal ball clear," said the genie.

The man used his last wish. "I wish that all my problems that had come from using this magic lamp would be erased."

The genie granted it as the way Agnes said to grant it. "I grant you your wish and restore your life back to the way it was before."

The man thanked her. "Oh thank you, thank you. I am deeply indebted to you."

"As my services are no longer required I shall retire into the lamp as you madam have instructed," said the genie.

Agnes waved her fingers around the man's clothes. At the same time that she cleaned up the man, she placed a memory gap spell on him. Agnes thought it was wise to keep her witch business to herself. The man left the shop after he purchased a very expensive bronze statue of a fairy for his garden.

The genie stayed in the lamp and was not freed to face a Witch's Council. Agnes placed the lamp on the top shelf with a sign saying, "Not for Sale." And there it sat for years, undisturbed.

Whenever Agnes left the shop in Harriet's care, Harriet changed the sign on the lamp to read "For Rent."

One day, a woman wearing an imported, mixed print, two-piece sleeveless top with a ruffled skirt to match and peep-toe platform pumps entered the Hidden Quiddity. The unusual oddities in the shop intrigued her. She delighted herself in the magic wands, potion bottles, old brooms, and the sort. What really caught her eye was the old, tarnished oil lamp sitting on the top shelf.

"Excuse me, why does the sign say 'For Rent'?" asked the curious, overdressed woman.

Smirking to herself, Harriet simply said, "When you are done with it, bring it back."

The woman, amused with the candor, laughed. "I'll take it."

The woman asked, "Please wrap the lamp carefully, and box it with extra packing. I wouldn't want anything to happen to it."

In the back of the shop, Harriet placed it in a box stuffed with newspaper and said to the lamp, "Have fun with this one."

When the woman got home, she placed the oil lamp on her coffee table and said, "This old lamp will make a nice conversation piece. Oh, but it is covered with gray tarnish. We can't have this wonderful lamp looking like this."

The woman went to her cleaning cupboard and pulled out metal polish and a cloth. She applied metal polish from the oil lamp's tip to the elegant handle and allowed it to dry. She began using the cloth at the tip and methodically rubbed in a circle motion. When the woman polished the main body of the lamp, she noticed that it heated up.

The woman set the lamp back down on the coffee table. Multicolored smoke rose out of the lamp's tip. The woman sat back against the couch. She stared at the form that had materialized and feared for her life.

"I am the genie of the lamp. Who are you?" bellowed the genie. "Who are you?"

"I … I'm Leslie."

"Leslie, I will grant you three wishes. Be careful for what you wish for," said the genie. "When you are ready for your first wish, rub the lamp."

With that, the genie disappeared back into the lamp.

A few days later, Leslie was on her knees next to the coffee table. Her hair was extremely unkempt. Her face looked as if she hasn't slept in days. Leslie's clothes were soiled and torn. Desperately, she rubbed the lamp. Bellowed out of the lamp's tip the multicolored smoke came.

"Are you ready for your second wish?" asked the genie.

"I want everything to return back before my first wish," said Leslie with a dry scratchy voice.

"It is done," said the genie.

Two weeks had gone by when Leslie again was on her knees next to the coffee table. Her hair was extremely unkempt. Her face looked as if she hadn't slept in weeks. Leslie's clothes were soiled and torn. Desperately, she rubbed the lamp. Bellowed out of the lamp's tip, the multicolored smoke came.

"Are you ready for your second wish?" asked the genie.

"I want everything to return back before my first wish," said Leslie in a dry, scratchy voice.

"It is done," said the genie.

After two near-disasters and another opportunity to try again, Leslie was on her knees next to the coffee table. She rubbed the lamp with anticipated haste. Bellowed out of the lamp as a tornado and a hurricane slammed together, the genie came.

"Ah, you are ready for your first wish," said the genie.

Leslie, still in her imported thermal union sleep suit and microfleece slippers, stood up. "I want to see the future."

"It is done," said the genie, fading back into the lamp quietly.

"I don't feel any different," Leslie thought.

Leslie prepared herself for the day. She put on her makeup and did her hair. She picked out a shimmering red dress with an Italian label and shoes to match. As she headed to the shopping mall, she noticed the car in front of her.

She thought, "They're going to run the red light."

Leslie pulled over to the side of the road. The car ran the red light, and a large pickup truck that had come across the intersection careened into it. Both vehicles were intertwined in a mangled mess, engulfed in flames.

At the shopping mall, Leslie walked by a newspaper rack. On the front of the paper was a photo of the car crash. She fumbled through her purse. She found some change to buy the paper.

"The date ... The date is tomorrow!" said Leslie.

Leslie sat at a mall eatery booth. Leslie turned the pages of the paper, noting events. She saw a large article about a local man who died the day before of a heart attack while shopping at the local mall. Next to the article was a photograph of the man.

Leslie looked up from the paper and thought, "I wonder what I could possibly do to stop this."

She then saw the man standing in line with a little girl to buy cookies. She grabbed the section of the newspaper with the article and took the paper over to him.

"Read this!" said Leslie, as she handed the man the newspaper.

The man held up the paper. "I don't know this person."

Leslie looked at the paper while the man was holding it. The article and date had changed to today.

Leslie said to the man, "I saw it. It was right there. Your obituary."

"Hey, look, this kind of joke isn't funny," said the man, pushing the paper back at Leslie.

Leslie stepped back and walked away. She dropped the paper to the floor and left the murmurs of other people in the food court behind. To clear her mind, Leslie stopped in a designer fashion store. She removed a scarlet, hooded toggle with welt pockets from the new style section.

A salesperson asked, "Do you need any help?"

"How much is this coat?" asked Leslie.

"Four hundred dollars. On sale today," replied the saleswoman.

"Oh, I'll wait until this weekend to buy it at the after-fire sale," exclaimed Leslie.

"What did you say?" asked the saleswoman.

Leslie thought for a second, "What did I say?"

She put the coat back on the rack. "Nothing. Nothing at all."

Leslie walked away.

At home, Leslie sat on the couch. She stared at the oil lamp, deep in thought. She hadn't decided what her second wish should be. Her first wish had caused so much trouble.

That night, she fell into a deep sleep on the couch. The next morning, a knock on her door came early. Leslie was wearing the same clothes from the day before. She looked out the window.

Police were standing outside her door. Leslie opened the door slowly and only as far as the chain lock allowed.

"Sorry to disturb you so early, miss, but we'd like to ask you a few questions. If you please, we need you down at the police station," said the policeman.

"What is this about?" asked Leslie.

"Everything will be explained to you down at the station," replied the policeman.

At the station, behind a two-way mirror, the saleswoman said, "Yes, that's her who said it."

Leslie sat in a room with a table and a couple of chairs.

A detective asked, "What do you know about a fire at the department store in the shopping mall?"

"I don't know anything about a fire," said Leslie.

"Didn't you say to a salesperson yesterday that you would buy the coat at the after-fire sale?" asked the detective.

"Well, yes. But what I meant was the price was too high and I would wait to buy it," explained Leslie.

"After the fire!" interjected the detective.

"A … A figure of speech," stuttered Leslie.

She was let go due to the fact she was nowhere near the mall at the time the fire was set, and they caught the arsonist who had no idea who Leslie was. She went home, sat on the couch, and looked at the lamp once again.

A knock on the door interrupted Leslie's train of thought of what her second wish should be. At the door was a woman with a little girl.

"How did you know?" demanded the woman.

Leslie looked at the woman and then at the little girl, the same little girl who was with the old man at the mall.

"I … I just … knew. That's all," replied Leslie. "I was trying to warn him."

"Well, I hope you have a good lawyer. My daughter was standing right there when her grandfather died yesterday. She kept saying that you did it," the woman spoke arrogantly to Leslie.

Leslie slammed the door shut and locked it.

That week, Leslie didn't leave her house. She stopped watching the news because they said the next day's date. Images filled her head. She couldn't sleep. She finally left her home and went for a drive to try to relax. Everywhere she looked, images entered her mind about the people around her.

Leslie stopped the car in the middle of the road and screamed, "Stop it! Stop it! Stop it!"

The cars around her honked their horns. Leslie got out of her car, leaving it in the middle of the street. Dazed and confused, she ran between the cars. She bumped into cars and caught her clothing on them. Material ripped as she pulled away. She collapsed at a nearby park, falling into the dirt and gravel of a playground. Leslie tried to get up and stumbled across wet grass and small mud puddles.

Leslie had fallen near a picnic area, where a boy suddenly stood over her. As Leslie stared into JayCee's eyes, in her mind, she saw an old man with sheer determination etched in his face. His voice rang in Leslie's ears.

"No! No! I won't do it. You're wrong about your future!" screamed Leslie.

She pushed herself up off the ground and made her way out of the park. She tried to get a grip on her situation. She found her way home, tired and exhausted. Once inside, she fell to the floor.

Leslie was on her knees next to the coffee table. Her hair was extremely unkempt. Her face looked as if she hadn't slept in a month. Her clothes were soiled and torn. Desperately, she rubbed the lamp. Bellowed out of the lamp, the multicolored smoke came.

"You are ready for your second wish?" asked the genie.

"I don't want to know the future anymore," cried Leslie in a dry, scratchy voice.

"It is done," said the genie. "Are you ready for your third wish?"

"Yes!" she replied. "I want you and your lamp to go back where I got you from and to leave me alone."

On the top shelf at the Hidden Quiddity, the old oil lamp showed back up. The sign leaning up against it said, "Not for Sale." Agnes noticed how newly polished it was.

"Harriet? Did you let this lamp out again?" asked Agnes.

"That was over a month ago," said Harriet. "It finally came back?"

And there the lamp sat on the top shelf, slowly beginning to tarnish once again.

Chapter Seventeen
JayCee and the
Sunshine Command

After the dinner with the Münters, Agnes went home to the Hidden Quiddity. She sat in her reading room where the crystal ball sat. It was still blackened out. She didn't get any information that helped her make the connection between Franklin and JayCee.

Thinking aloud, Agnes said, "I need your advice, Grandpa."

That's when it came to her. Agnes had hoped the meeting of the two families allowed JayCee to have dinner and possibly other evening activities in the near future. To start with, she needed JayCee that very next night.

Penelope still questioned the day's events. She really liked JayCee. The adult talk of her being JayCee's one true love, however, overwhelmed her. Late that night, Penelope stood in front of the scrying mirror with her arms stretched out. Both her index and middle fingers were pointing at her image. She crossed her right fingers first. There stood her father in the reflection of the mirror. Penelope then switched her crossed fingers to her left hand. In the mirror were her mother and father together. Agnes walked up behind Penelope and gently placed her hands on her shoulders.

"It won't work the same for you," said Agnes.

"You were born a witch. Your powers are set by bloodline, whereas JayCee's powers were acquired through magical manipulation. And, yes, some comes from you, too. Love is the most magical power there is, and it must be handled wisely," stated Agnes, anticipating Penelope's question.

"I have black magic powers. My father's image appeared when I crossed my right fingers," said Penelope.

"We all have some black magic power. Haven't you ever wanted to cast a bad spell on someone who did something to you?" asked Agnes.

Penelope nodded her head sadly while she thought of a time she almost did out of revenge.

"You're still wondering if JayCee is your true love, aren't you," asked Agnes. "What do you feel?"

"I … I don't know. I'm confused." Penelope said, beginning to cry. Agnes held her. "I think I love him, Agnes. I don't want to hurt him if I'm wrong."

Agnes then handed a book to Penelope. "Read this book. Try to learn from this woman's mistake."

Penelope took the book from Agnes and read the title aloud, "Camelot."

The morning after the dinner with the Candlewicks, JayCee was in the kitchen eating breakfast while waiting for Penelope. He had forgotten to make a meeting place with her the night before. He figured she would show up. The morning passed, and Penelope still had not appeared. He didn't know where they lived since Penelope took them there by magic.

"You're not going to see Penelope today?" asked JayCee's mom.

"I'm leaving soon," said JayCee.

JayCee walked out the front door and headed over to the large tree. He hoped something magical would have happen. But he had a thought. He decided to use the phone book to find her. Not wanting to go back inside, JayCee remembered about moving the plates. He had better control with his left hand. He raised his left hand, pointed at the house with his two fingers, and concentrated on the phone book. It floated right to him.

Stuck in between some pages were shards of glass. JayCee looked back at the kitchen window. One of the panes was broken. He didn't see his mom looking out.

First, he looked in the white pages under Candlewick. Then he ran his finger down through candle factory, candlelight, and Candlewood. No Candlewick. He tried the Hidden Quiddity under "H" and "Q."

JayCee thumbed through the yellow pages, not really knowing what to look under. He tried under witchcraft, wireless phones, and woodcraft. No witch anything.

"Harriet, would you open the shop by herself this morning? I want to talk to Cindy Münter alone. Maybe she might remember seeing McDermit. But I first need to see Florence," said Agnes.

"I guess I could handle it alone. You know Lughnassadh is in a couple of days," reminded Harriet.

"I'll be back before the rush hit. I'm just going to show this photo that James Candlewick sent me of Franklin McDermit," said Agnes as she headed out the door.

Penelope was still in her bedroom. She stayed up late and read the book that Agnes gave her. Penelope was still crying. Sunshine flew around, trying to get Penelope to open her hands.

"No, Sunshine, I don't want any pixie dust today."

Penelope pulled the covers over her head. Sunshine tried again and again.

"Leave me alone, please," cried Penelope.

JayCee was getting frustrated. He had no idea where or how to find Penelope. An insect came buzzing around his head. He tried to swat it with his hands, but missed. Then he realized it was a little person with violet, feather duster-type wings; pointed ears; big green eyes; and bright orange hair.

"Sunshine?" asked JayCee, not knowing pixies did not talk. He looked around for Penelope, but she wasn't there.

"Sunshine, where is Penelope?" asked JayCee. "Can you take me to her?"

Sunshine flew around JayCee's head until he said Penelope's name. At that point, she stopped in front of JayCee and gestured. JayCee did not understand.

"You can take me to Penelope. Show me how," asked JayCee.

Sunshine pointed at JayCee and then counted with her fingers. One, two, three. Then she made a circular motion with her right hand with two fingers pointed up. JayCee stood there confused. Sunshine did it again.

"You want me to count to three and then wave my fingers in a circle?" asked JayCee. "How will that get me to Penelope?"

At the sound of Penelope's name, Sunshine excitedly counted on her fingers. One, two, three. Then she swirled her fingers in a circle.

JayCee said, "I should say Penelope three times and swirl my fingers in a circle. That will take me to her?"

Sunshine flew around JayCee as her way of saying yes. JayCee stood there and held his right hand up with two fingers pointing up.

"Penelope, Penelope, Penelope," JayCee said. Then he circled his fingers.

A whirlwind spun around JayCee, picking him up. It was cold, not like when he and Penelope did it. It spun around and moved over houses and trees, flying JayCee through the air.

"In addition to it being cold, this also took longer," thought JayCee.

Agnes finished talking to Florence, who now resided in a rest home, as she was much older than the first time they met. Florence did not see that man in the photo at all that night in the maternity ward.

Agnes then appeared at the front door of the Münter's house and rang the doorbell.

When Cindy answered the door, Agnes asked, "Can I come in and talk to you?"

"Would you like some coffee?" asked Cindy.

Cindy and Agnes went into the kitchen, where Agnes saw the broken windowpane. She saw the whirlwind sweeping up JayCee. Not knowing exactly how the window became broken, Agnes knew it would distract Cindy's attention. Without drawing attention, Agnes pointed at the broken window with two fingers.

Agnes showed Cindy the picture of Franklin McDermit. "Have you ever seen this man?"

"No, I've never seen him before," said Cindy. "What is this about?"

Agnes went into detail about McDermit's disappearance about the same time that JayCee was born. She told the story of the diaper changing witnessed by Nurse Florence. Agnes referred to the paper bag trick that JayCee used to do when he was a little boy.

"McDermit is a wizard, Cindy," admitted Agnes. "He passed magical powers to JayCee somehow and then disappeared thirteen years ago. I am trying to figure out the connection. This connection between them is what will help me find McDermit or at least determine what happened to him."

Cindy asked, "And you are a—"

"Witch," Agnes said, finishing her sentence.

"And your sister?" asked Cindy.

"A witch also," stated Agnes.

"But certainly not your cousin Penelope," said Cindy.

"Oh, yes, she is a witch, too," said Agnes.

"Please don't harm JayCee," pleaded Cindy.

Agnes calmed Cindy's fears. "JayCee is fine. However, he is in danger because of the connection to McDermit's disappearance thirteen years ago."

"Cindy, we love JayCee dearly, and we're trying to help him. That is why I am here telling you all this," explained Agnes, taking

Cindy's hand to comfort her. That was when she realized that Cindy had been spelled.

"When did you meet a witch before?" asked Agnes.

"I never met a witch before you. You're the first one," said Cindy.

"You have had a spell put on you," cautioned Agnes.

Harriet passed by Penelope's room and heard her crying.

"Penelope?" called Harriet.

"Go away," cried Penelope.

Harriet opened the door and went in. On the floor was the book, *Camelot*. The page was opened to where Lady Gwenivere had caused the fall of King Arthur.

"I've never seen you cry since you've been here. Where is your pixie?" asked Harriet.

Penelope didn't answer.

"Tell me what's wrong. Maybe I can help," said Harriet.

Penelope pulled down the covers. "I'm JayCee's true love, and only I can keep him safe from black magic. If I hurt his feelings, it will be my fault that he turns to the black magic side. I … I can't … be. This is too much for me." She continued to cry.

"I heard you tried to use the mirror test to see if JayCee is your true love."

The door to the shop opened, and someone came in.

"Maybe that's Agnes with some good news," said Harriet.

Harriet left Penelope to check who came in the shop. She came quickly back to Penelope's bedroom.

"I can't give you the answer if JayCee is your true love, but someone else can," exclaimed Harriet.

"Who is it?" Penelope asked.

"You'll have to get dressed and come out to the shop," Harriet said, acting like the mischievous witch she was. She pulled the blankets off Penelope and the bed. "Get up, Penelope."

With tears still running down her face, Penelope got dressed and came out to the shop. Standing there was JayCee with Sunshine sitting on his left shoulder. Penelope stared at JayCee and Sunshine, who held onto JayCee's neck with her right arm. Sunshine leaned over, kissed JayCee on the neck, and then flew in front of him, motioning him to open his hands. She sprinkled pixie dust in his hands. Sunshine then pointed to Penelope's face.

JayCee walked over to Penelope and rubbed the pixie dust on her face. Penelope's sadness slowly faded like darkness at sunrise.

"I think you got your answer," said Harriet.

JayCee and Penelope hugged each other.

"Please promise me that you'll never use black magic," pleaded Penelope.

"Okay, break it up," said Harriet. "Why don't the two of you go and act like thirteen-year-olds and find a park to play in?"

Agnes had Cindy lay down on the couch in the living room.

"Sleep. Sleep quietly. Dream," whispered Agnes. "Diddly dyne go back in time. Tell me what spell to find."

Cindy slowly said, "I can't remember."

Agnes thought to herself, "I should have known. A disrembra spell."

"Rosey posey flippin flu, remember what you once knew," said Agnes.

Cindy said, "Who are you? Where's Dr. Vandle?"

"What do you see, Cindy?" asked Agnes.

"A man with brown hair wearing a surgical mask that's covering his long, brown beard," said Cindy. "What are you doing with my baby?"

"What is the man doing?" asked Agnes.

"He is holding a bottle to my baby's mouth," said Cindy.

"What is in the bottle, Cindy?" asked Agnes.

"Nothing," said Cindy. "My baby is breathing into it."

"First breath," said Agnes. "Sleep quietly, Cindy. Remember nothing I have told you."

Agnes walked Cindy into the kitchen and sat her down at the table. Agnes snapped her fingers and started talking in mid-sentence. "They're enjoying each other's company so much I thought it would be nice to take them on a picnic today if that is all right with you?"

Cindy stared at Agnes for a foggy moment. "Oh. Oh, yes. Yes, of course. That sounds great."

"Well, thank you for the coffee. I'll see myself out," said Agnes as she got up from the table. She walked to the front door and disappeared without opening it.

Penelope and JayCee walked outside and looked up and down the street.

JayCee asked, "If I tell you of a park, can you take us there?"

"Only if it is in Broomstick," said Penelope.

"Would you like to meet my friends from school?" asked JayCee.

"Oh, yes, I would," said Penelope.

"You know they're nonmagical and have never seen a witch," cautioned JayCee.

"I better tell Harriet where we are going," Penelope said.

She went back into the potion shop and came right back out.

JayCee held Penelope's hands. But, this time, JayCee kept his eyes open while Penelope transported them to the park. JayCee saw the whole world spin around them as if time itself had shifted into high gear. As quickly as the warming sensation came, it was gone. JayCee and Penelope were standing in the park. JayCee noticed he was standing over a woman who was lying on the grass. The woman stared up into JayCee's eyes.

She suddenly started screaming, "No! No! I won't do it. You're wrong about your future."

Then the woman pushed herself up off the ground. JayCee watched as she made her way out of the park.

"What was that all about?" asked Penelope.

"I have no idea," said JayCee.

As JayCee and Penelope walked, JayCee asked, "What makes your way of taking us places so different than what Sunshine had me do?"

"I came here by dragon's breath. As long as I am here, I can use it, but only in Broomstick," explained Penelope. "This was my father's way of restricting my travel."

"Sunshine probably used the easiest method she could show you because she doesn't talk," suggested Penelope.

When Agnes returned to the Hidden Quiddity, Harriet told her about Penelope and JayCee and what Sunshine did.

"Where are they now?" asked Agnes.

"They went to meet JayCee's friends at a park near his house," stated Harriet.

Agnes grabbed Harriet's arm and bolted out of the shop.

"What! What did I say?" asked Harriet.

Agnes dragged Harriet into the Poison Apple.

She said, "Bee, I need two dozen finger niblets, three dozen spider legs, and a cask of rich foamy carbonated witch hazelnut soda to go quickly."

"What's the matter with you, Agnes?" asked Harriet.

"I told Cindy we were taking them on a picnic today," explained Agnes.

With lunch in their arms, Agnes and Harriet winked out of the Poison Apple. They caught up with JayCee and Penelope at the park. They were throwing a ball around. Penelope was wearing a giant leather hand to catch it. Agnes found a table and laid out the food.

Harriet went over to the kids playing. "We have lunch over here for you and your friends."

JayCee, Penelope, and four of JayCee's friends came over to the table.

One of the boys looked at the food. "What is it?"

"Finger niblets and spider legs," said Harriet.

JayCee whispered to his friends, "They own a novelty shop and make food look strange for fun. It's pigs in a blanket and chicken strips."

While the kids enjoyed the food and rich foamy carbonated witch hazelnut soda, Cindy happened to come over. She had been walking through the park, trying to clear her head.

"If I knew this was where you would be having your picnic, I would have made up some food and joined you," said Cindy.

Agnes said, "I'm sorry. JayCee picked the park because his friends are here."

Cindy looked at the food. "Um, this looks interesting."

She picked up a finger niblet. "This would be something you would serve at a Halloween party," said Cindy as she took a bite.

"Oh, we do," said Harriet, not realizing Cindy's implication.

Agnes pulled Cindy off to the side to speak to her.

She said, "We're having a sleepover this evening for some of the small children in our neighborhood. We sure could use JayCee's help. Of course, the older kids will be well chaperoned."

"I guess it will be all right. Can I get your phone number? I noticed our phone book was missing earlier when I wanted to look up your novelty shop," said Cindy.

Agnes gave Cindy a magical phone number that, if called, would let Agnes know Cindy was calling her.

After the picnic was over, Agnes told JayCee that his mom was allowing him to spend the night with them. JayCee ran home and packed an overnight bag, kissed his mom on the cheek, and ran back to the park. The four of them disappeared from the park and went back to the Hidden Quiddity.

"Why is your way different from Penelope's and the way Sunshine showed me?" asked JayCee, trying to understand magic.

"We were born here," said Harriet.

"So was I," said JayCee.

"Yes, but do you know where you are going?" asked Harriet.

"I need to talk to you about a broken window, JayCee," said Agnes.

JayCee explained how he tried to find them.

He said, "So I levitated the phone book out of the house. When I looked back, the window was broken."

"You should not be doing magic. You do not have control of this power. This power controls you. A broken window is minor compared to what damage you could inflict by doing magic. It is nothing to play with," warned Agnes.

When Agnes had a moment alone with Harriet, she explained what went on with Cindy.

"I found out today what Franklin was doing and how JayCee became involved. From this point on, I need JayCee's and Penelope's full cooperation to keep all of us safe," stated Agnes, now fully concerned. "I'll explain over supper what we are going to do tonight."

At the Poison Apple, Agnes asked the tavern keep for use of the back room and for Bee to be their hostess. Sitting in the back room, Agnes began to explain that the parchment that Franklin had found in the London Library was hidden under the cover of a journal that a sorcerer named Oozar had written.

"The parchment must have a powerful magical spell of some kind because I know Franklin acquired ice and water samples destined for the Russian Academy of Science from Lake Vostok in Antarctica and a newborn baby's first breath," explained Agnes.

"Am I the baby he acquired that first breath from?" asked JayCee.

"That is what I found out today. Franklin was the one who delivered you and then captured your first breath in a bottle. He used a memory-erasing spell on your parents, but memories are never really erased. They're just forgotten. It is what Franklin McDermit did with your first breath that made the connection between you, Oozar the Sorcerer, and Franklin's disappearance thirteen years ago."

"I'm not really a wizard of any kind. I was being exploited for his own personal gain for magical power," said JayCee, now deeply upset.

"That may have been Franklin's intentions in using your first breath, but not to have any harm come to you. Something must have gone terribly wrong, and Oozar's black magical power was transferred to you by mistake," said Agnes. "Now it seems that Franklin has been trying to stop Oozar's black magic from doing something to you these past thirteen years. The older you become, the stronger the black magic grows within you. Until Penelope gave you the ability to control the black magic, it was trying to get you to do something for Oozar. Now, through the love you two have for each other that power has been subdued for the time being."

Harriet interrupted, "I can't believe that Franklin was trying to gain black magic power from a long-dead sorcerer. That doesn't sound like the Franklin McDermit I knew. But, then again, he did turn you away Agnes, possibly for that reason."

Agnes stared at Harriet with hardened eyes. "He didn't turn me away, Harriet. I was too young to be thinking of love.

Chapter Eighteen
Oozar,
the Wizard's Apprentice

Oozar came from a family with limited magical power. His parents had wanted him to have the best training available. At a very young age, Oozar was taken to a very powerful wizard, and he was sold into servitude as a wizard's apprentice.

Oozar lived in the castle's dungeon located in the valley of Dragonstep. He labored at the filthiest jobs imagined. When the master wizard taught him how to read and write, Oozar began to study the master's journals intensely. Down in the dungeon, he practiced various methods of extracting potent ingredients from their source. Fermentation, distillation, fractionation, and substance exchange methods were described in full detail in this one journal.

There were various journals on how to grow plants for healing potions and what parts were used. It described the use of herbs, roots, and berries and what extraction method worked the best. One journal Oozar read had listed plants to avoid for various reasons. Some were poisonous plants that caused ill effects. Other plants could cause behavior changes. Oozar kept his own journal of this information hidden from the master wizard.

While the master wizard slept, Oozar experimented on rats that he would catch in the dungeon. With one plant that caused behavior change, he made a potion and forced a rat to swallow it. Watching intently, Oozar made notes of the effects and actions of the rat. Within an hour, the rat had gnawed all of his appendages off and then died.

At his young age, Oozar knew the only way he'd ever be a powerful wizard was through the art of black magic. Whenever the master wizard taught him a spell, Oozar wrote it down carefully. When he was by himself, he studied the spell, word by word. Oozar figured out where changes were to be made and which inflected the most harm or conjured up a violent infestation upon someone.

Oozar caught a gnome as he swept a passageway alone and tested one of his spells on the unsuspecting creature. The gnome gasped for air. Boiling blisters burst and oozed pus from his skin. After the gnome was dead, Oozar used a spell that covered up his dastardly deed. He sent the body of his victim into a fiery kiln and turned his victim into ashes.

Every morning, Oozar carried the master wizard's breakfast tray into his sleeping chamber. Oozar sat the tray on a table and then wakened the master wizard.

"Master, sir," called Oozar. "Master?"

On this particular morning, Oozar found his master had died in his sleep the night before. It had been about twenty solar cycles since Oozar had first come to the castle. Oozar went downstairs to the big hall and started a fire in the main fireplace. Elves dragged the dead master's body to the fireplace. For the next three days and nights, Oozar axed off pieces of his master's body and fed the parts into the fire. As more wood was set in the fireplace, the flame showed a gruesome figure with blood splattered on his robe and face. Oozar incinerated the old wizard to ashes. During this time, wizards and witches of the valley noticed the rolling black smoke that came from the castle and inquired about it.

Oozar told them, "Master Wizard is experimenting with new potions and will soon share the news with all of you."

"I don't like this," said one witch to another. "Something is not right."

Others believed Oozar was hiding something.

"I demand to see your master," stated a wizard.

"I'm sorry. Master has left word not to be disturbed for any reason," Oozar lied to the wizard.

By the second day, Oozar had envelopes. He handed them out as more people came to the castle.

"An invitation to a party," Oozar said.

Finally, after three days and nights, the wizard's body had completely burned to ash. After the fire had gone out and cooled, Oozar sifted through the ashes.

"Ah, I found it," announced Oozar.

He picked out the glowing jade amulet. He held it up to the light that came from a window and peered through it. Laughter echoed through the castle as he clutched the amulet in his hands. It was now rightfully his. His apprenticeship had ended. He felt the magical power of the old wizard as the power of the amulet surged through his body.

The night of the party, wizards and witches from the town of Dragonstep and the surrounding valley came dressed in their finest robes. A large buffet table extended from one end of the great hall to the other. Elves served and catered to the needs of the guest. A stringed quartet of elves played happy little tunes. Gnomes kept the hall clean of dirty dishes and garbage. At the entrance was Oozar, playing the humbled wizard's apprentice greeted the incoming guests.

"My master welcomes you to his home," Oozar said, bowing like a servant. "Enjoy the food and drink provided."

Simple chitchat filled the great hall while everyone feasted and drank. Some even danced to the music played by the elf quartet. Eventually, the conversation turned to the question of the host's location.

"Please be patient. He will join us soon," said Oozar.

Oozar slipped out of the hall and went into a nearby study. There, he changed into his former master's best robe and traditional hat. In his hand was the wand of the old wizard.

With a flash, tongues of flamed fire bellowed green smoke as Oozar appeared in the great hall.

"The old wizard is dead. I am now Oozar the Sorcerer."

Whispers circled the hall, "Did he call himself a sorcerer?"

"He must have killed the wizard."

"No, if he did, he wouldn't have been able to absorb his power."

Many headed for the way out. But a wall of multicolored flames blocked the way.

"You fear me. That is good, so you should fear me. I am now the law of the land," said Oozar.

Three wizards pulled out their wands and attacked with curses. However, Oozar anticipated this, and he was ready for them. He hit them with a curse so awful that it left three bubbled, blistered globs of flesh and bone that reeked with the odor of abandoned, unfertile, rotten dragon eggs.

"I need an apprentice. You there," said Oozar, pointing at a young boy. "You will serve my purpose."

The boy's father quickly stood between Oozar and his son. He said, "You will not take my boy as an apprentice to learn your wretched sorcerer's ways!"

Two more bubbled globs lay on the floor with the same stench as the other three.

"Then you!" exclaimed Oozar, now pointing at a young witch with long, coal black hair, gray eyes, and pale white skin. "I will have you as my apprentice, or everyone here dies!"

With the fate of all placed on her, the young witch slowly walked over to Oozar. She kneeled down on her knees and bowed her head. She whispered, "Please do not kill them. I will do whatever you ask."

"How old are you?" asked Oozar.

The young witch looked back at her parents and then turned her head toward Oozar.

She looked up at him and answered, "About nineteen summers, my master."

Oozar peered into the young witch's eyes. In a softened voice, he asked, "What is your name?"

"Vigoda Whetstone, my master," she replied.

Oozar felt a twinge of weakness in his black magical power as if another more powerful magical force had invaded his soul. Oozar bent down to Vigoda's left ear.

For the first time in his life, he spoke with a kindly voice, "For you, Miss Whetstone, they can all leave."

The wall of flames diminished. Except for Vigoda's parents, all the guests left the castle quietly.

Vigoda turned her head toward her parents and pleaded, "Please go now. You'll only wind up like those who have already resisted him. Please go." Then she turned her head back to Oozar's direction and stared silently at the stone floor.

Quietly, Vigoda's parents walked out of the great hall with Mr. Whetstone's arm wrapped around his wife's shoulders. Outside, Vigoda's mother began to weep.

Through the years, Oozar made progress as he refined his black magic. His studies had him traveling to many parts of the known world. From the jungles of the African continent, he brought back the art of voodoo, which used effigies of his enemies. While Oozar studied Asian cults, he learned meditation. Oozar entered the minds of nonmagical people and used them for dangerous tasks that ended in a gruesome death. The biggest discovery for Oozar was from the Greeks. He found the four elements of the universe held a mysterious power. Oozar studied each one separately.

Fire, as common it may be, had the greatest influence on the mind. It could not be held nor touched. It was translucent. It destroyed whatever it came in contact with. Yet, when kept small, it appeared soft and kind, fluid in motion.

Earth was solid and hard. It was held in one's hand. Earth took various shapes and colors. It was used in many ways. Oozar noted that, when fire was combined with earth, fire turned the Earth molten hot.

Air was taken for granted. Like fire, it could not be held. It was transparent. It had a spiritual presence in that it moved freely and wasn't tied to anything. It was almost ghostly. Fire could not burn without it.

Water was deep with mystery. Like the earth, it was found solid. Water turned into the ghostlike quality of air when fire was indirectly connected to it. Water killed fire. It made earth molten, but it was not harmful. Air traveled through water, but only in the up direction. Water cleansed the universe of unwanted spirits.

The one thing Oozar noted was that the four elements were never combined together at the same time, except maybe at the beginning of time.

"What power would there be if all four were somehow triggered to fuse together as one?" Oozar questioned himself.

Trial and error led the way for Oozar as he attempted to combine earth, water, air, and fire. Purity of these elements turned out to be his biggest problem. Age of the elements had become a questionable factor. They had to be as close to the beginning of the universe as possible. The search for the oldest ingredients led Oozar to Iceland. Through meditation, Oozar used the local townspeople. They collected deep blue ice and molten rock. He had them fly brooms while wearing clothing intertwined with gold thread into the mysterious dancing lights.

The air kept him at bay. Early experiments rendered poor results because no triggered action occurred. Oozar decided he needed air that was alive at one time. He collected the last breath of a dying man who lived a long life.

Up in one of the towers of the castle where Oozar conducted his experiments, he combined the molten rock, deep blue ice, powder of the clothing that collected the dancing lights, and the last breath of the dying man in a large cauldron. Blue smoke bellowed and rolled over and out of the cauldron, heading down to the stone floor. A vortex swirled opened inside the cauldron.

Oozar used this vortex beyond anyone's imagination. He conjured up the dead. He made potions with ingredients that did not normally combine together. The most powerful use was that Oozar had the ability to see into the future. Not just the near future, but eons yet to come. The images were strange and foreign. Oozar assumed this powerful vortex destined him to immortality and the future. He was half-right.

On a large parchment, Oozar wrote the steps he had done with the elements. He described in detail where he collected them and how he had combined them together. In his own handwriting, he told of how he used the vortex to perform the blackest of magic. The last part was written about the ultimate experiment for immortality and power he was about to do.

Oozar folded the parchment and slipped it behind his personal journal's front leather cover for safekeeping, where he could find it in the future if needed. With the secret hidden away, with his wand, Oozar drew the vortex away from the cauldron and transferred it to his chest. Violently, the vortex swirled within him. It pulled his soul, spirit, and power into the center of the vortex. His body burst into flames inside his sorcerer's robe. As Oozar fell back onto the stone floor, the vortex returned to the cauldron and vanished. What lay there was a charred skeleton within a smoldering robe and a burnt wand. Oozar got his immortality. He was at the end of time in the cold, dead universe, void of all energy and matter.

Vigoda was limited to what magic she had learned and used. When Oozar was away, she kept a closely guarded journal of any magical information she found without being discovered by enchantments or charms that protected Oozar's books.

She also visited her parents and learned from them until they passed away. Vigoda protected herself from Oozar by keeping her parents' amulets in a safe place. She did not absorb them into her own magical power.

As time went on, Vigoda bore three sons with Oozar. She kept the name of Whetstone and passed it on to her sons. Through them, Oozar's black magic was passed on to their heirs.

Vigoda discovered Oozar's charred remains in the tower. But his magical amulet, which was usually left behind when one died, wasn't there. She lived out her life in the castle. Even though she never bothered anyone or did any black magic, Vigoda Whetstone was labeled a sorceress since she was willing to be his apprentice and supposedly inherited his power.

This position had given her great power without using any magic at all. Ironically, the wizarding world remembered Vigoda Whetstone the Sorceress. Oozar faded into nothingness, hardly more than a mythical folklore about a terrible sorcerer.

Chapter Nineteen
The Séance

When Jay Münter came home from work, he wasn't too pleased with the way the day went, and this night wasn't starting off any better. He found the phone book in the yard by the large tree. When he picked up the phone book, he cut the palm of his right hand on the broken glass that stuck out of the pages.

The lights in the house were all off. With the outside ornamental lights on, the windows and front entrance were darkened, causing a shadowy, grim face that glared down at Jay. Once inside, he found Cindy sitting in the dark. She wasn't fully coherent from the day's events. Jay brought Cindy back to reality when he turned on the living room lights.

"What is going on?" asked Jay, as he stood with blood dripping on the carpet. "And where is JayCee? The yard work isn't done, and the trash isn't at the street for tomorrow."

Cindy got up from the couch, feeling a little off center. She tried to catch her balance and stumbled a little. She noticed Jay's hand was bleeding.

She asked, "What happened to your hand?"

"I cut it on glass that was sticking out of this phone book I found outside. Where's JayCee?" asked Jay.

"He's helping with a sleepover for some small kids with Agnes and Penelope," said Cindy.

"We still don't know where they live or have a phone number to reach them," explained Jay, a little upset.

"I have their phone number," said Cindy as her mind started to come out of her fog.

Bee had served up rich foamy carbonated witch hazelnut soda when Agnes asked her, "I need a medium tonight, Bee. Can you help me out?"

"Of course, dear, I'll get Elizabeth and Charmain to be my spirit guides," answered Bee.

In her ear, Agnes heard a phone ring. But it was Jay, not Cindy. Agnes quickly left the back room and went into the crowded tavern.

"Hello, Mr. Münter, how are you doing?" asked Agnes.

Jay, taken aback at Agnes's acknowledgment, said, "I don't think this is a good idea that JayCee is gone tonight. If you please, give me your address. I'll come right over to pick him up."

"I'm having a hard time hearing you with all the children around me. Let me call you back when I get into a quieter room," Agnes said, hanging up before Jay could reply.

Agnes pulled Bee over. "I need a big favor. JayCee's dad wants an address to come pick up his son. If he sees the Hidden Quiddity, I won't be able to get near JayCee to help him. I also need small kids to make it look like a party."

"Here's my house address. It's next door to the Browns, a nonmagical family," said Bee.

"I know their son, Brian," said Agnes.

Agnes walked back into the quiet back room with the information Bee had given her. She called Jay Münter back, using her magic with the phone system.

"Hello, Mr. Münter, this is Agnes. Sorry about the noise. I'm sorry you feel this isn't a good time for JayCee to stay over. So here's the address. It is next door to Robert Brown. Do you know him?"

When Agnes said the name Robert Brown, Jay's temper hit an all-time high. Jay paused and took in a couple of deep breaths before answering. "Yes, I know him. I'll be right over to pick up JayCee."

Agnes looked at everyone and urgently said, "We have to leave now!"

Bee, in the meantime, had gone over to a booth and talked to two wizards, one of them being Winston Wisestone. They popped out after their conversation with Bee.

"This is just great. The address Agnes gave me is next door to the guy who made my day miserable," complained Jay while Cindy bandaged his right hand. "Until three days ago, I was getting clear, concise finance records from this one division. Then H.G. White promotes a sales contract representative to production manager. I go over to his office to discuss the discrepancies in his ordering report, and he tells me someone named Stiltskins couldn't give him an accurate straw-into-gold ratio. Then he was explaining that Nymphs, whoever that guy is, wouldn't tell him the name of the company that the hand-braided rope comes from."

Jay rambled on about his bad day at work to Cindy.

Winston and the other wizard went through the neighborhood, gathered up the little ones, and set up a party atmosphere at Bee's house. Wanda came from the house on the other side of the Brown's place and assisted as well.

Agnes told JayCee, "No matter what is said, just go along with it. Don't say a word. I'll do all the talking."

When Agnes and the others arrived at Bee's house, JayCee saw Wanda Whetstone for the very first time. She was standing out front with the children.

He walked up to her. "I know you! You're Vigoda Whetstone."

Both Wanda and Penelope said together, "What did you just say?"

"I don't why I know this, but he loves you," said JayCee with a questionable look on his face.

"Who loves me?" asked Wanda.

JayCee stared at Wanda with glazed eyes and a somber expression on his face.

Almost with a different voice that sounded off in the distance, JayCee said to Wanda, "Oozar adores you with deep admiration. You bring sunshine into the deepest hollows of the grave. When he first set eyes upon you, he knew you had powerful magic that even he could not match. Oozar says he tried to give back love to you that you showed him. He just didn't know how."

Agnes noted that JayCee had spoken in present tense. "JayCee, are you referring to Wanda as Vigoda?"

"Yes. He loves Vigoda Whetstone," said JayCee, staring into Wanda's gray eyes.

"How is Vigoda the Sorceress and Oozar the Sorcerer connected?" asked Harriet.

Wanda spoke up, "I know. My parents have a copy of a Whetstone family tree that was found in Salem. Vigoda had three sons with a sorcerer named Oozar."

Even Penelope knew of Vigoda the Sorceress.

"Her castle sits empty on a hill that overlooks Dragonstep," said Penelope. "No one goes near it because of the black magic curse."

Agnes pulled JayCee away from Wanda. JayCee blinked his eye to focus them.

"I'm all right," JayCee said quietly to Agnes.

When Cindy and Jay arrived at the house, Agnes was at the front door. JayCee and Harriet stood inside the door, remaining out of sight. Penelope, Wanda, and the two adult wizards played a game with the children.

Jay noticed the house next door was the only one with a car sitting in the driveway. Jay and Cindy walked up to the front door where JayCee and Agnes were standing.

"I'm sorry for the inconvenience we may have caused you. After talking to Cindy this morning, I thought the two of you could use some time alone," Agnes said. "And we needed some help with this party."

"JayCee hasn't been doing his yard work, and tomorrow is trash day," said Jay in a slightly annoyed tone.

Harriet whispered to someone in the dark, "We need gnomes over there to do yard work and take out the trash."

"Prior to us coming over here from the park, JayCee said he needed some time to do the yard and get the trash out to the street," stated Agnes, emphasizing "yard" and "trash."

"Harriet and JayCee left here just prior to your phone call to take care of the yard and trash," said Agnes, again emphasizing "yard" and "trash." "Maybe you passed them on the way here." She had a smile on her face that made her pleasant as could be. "But, if JayCee needs to go home, we will bring him right over when he and Harriet get back."

Agnes paused while she smiled at Jay and Cindy, giving Harriet enough time to move. Holding JayCee by his shoulders, Harriet popped out of the house and stood right behind Jay and Cindy.

"Oh, JayCee and Harriet are here. Walking up the driveway now," exclaimed Agnes.

As if on cue, the children ran up to JayCee. "Mr. JayCee, can you teach us how to throw and catch a ball?"

"I'm sorry, children, but Mr. JayCee has to go home," said Agnes, wearing a sad face.

"Aw," said all of the children together.

About that same time, Robert Brown walked up the driveway to where Jay was standing.

Robert said, "You know these people and you act like you have no idea what I'm talking about at work?"

Jay looked at Robert with a disturbed look on his face.

Jay asked, "How does knowing your neighbors make any sense of what you were talking about at work? Wait. Let's just keep work at work. Okay, maybe I do need some quiet time. The yard work had better be done, JayCee, or your summer vacation is over."

"I can guarantee that it is done, Mr. Münter," said Harriet.

Agnes bent toward Jay and whispered, "Why don't you take Cindy out for dinner?"

Jay and Cindy got in their car and drove away, leaving JayCee with Agnes.

"What about the yard? When Dad sees I haven't gotten it done," said JayCee worriedly.

"It is already taken care of," said Harriet. She rubbed the top of JayCee's head.

Harriet turned to Agnes while gesturing toward where Jay had been. "Did you see that, Agnes? He had a cut across his life, finance, and love line all at the same time."

"What does it mean?" asked Penelope.

"A big change is coming in his life. A big, big change," explained Harriet. She stared off into space, as if seeing what was to come.

Once the ruse of a party was over Agnes, Harriet, Penelope, and JayCee stayed a short while and entertained the neighborhood children to thank them for their help. JayCee tossed a ball around with the youngsters. This actually surprised the adult wizards that something nonmagical as tossing an ordinary ball was really fun.

At one point, Agnes said, "It's time we went back to the Poison Apple."

Jay and Cindy went out to dinner at a small quiet café.

Jay asked, "Can you believe that setup? Agnes was doing all the talking. The children were coming up, as on cue. I bet they even had Robert Brown involved with his cockamamie story from earlier today. What do you think is really going on? And where was the car Harriet and JayCee arrived in?"

"Well, I think JayCee is trying to grow up a little," said Cindy.

"Still, something strange is going on," Jay reiterated.

After dinner, Jay and Cindy headed right back over to where JayCee was supposed to have been.

"Just as I thought," said Jay. "There is no one here."

Jay walked over to the Brown's house and rang the doorbell. When Robert opened the door, Jay walked into their house.

"All right, what is this scam going on next door that you are involved with? Starting with the shenanigans at work today," steamed Jay.

Robert said, "You barge into my house and demand to know what I am involved with? You! You're the one with those people as friends, allowing your son to fraternize with them."

"What do you mean? Those people?" demanded Jay.

"You know what those people are!" said Robert, pointing at Jay's chest.

"No, I don't," stated Jay, raising his voice.

Robert took a step back. "You really don't know, do you?"

"Just what in the world are you talking about?" asked Jay.

"Nothing. I said too much. Now, if you please, would you kindly leave my house," said Robert, returning his voice to its normal tone.

"Not until you tell me where my son is," Jay said, irritated.

"Why don't you try the Poison Apple two blocks over? Now get out of my house," demanded Robert.

Jay drove over to where Robert suggested. They drove down a dimly lit street without any vehicle traffic. Jay also noticed there wasn't any parking or any cars around anywhere to speak of. Jay and Cindy found the Poison Apple. Jay parked on the street right in front of the tavern. They both looked at the rounded log front.

Jay said, "This could be used as a backdrop of a medieval witch hunt movie."

"Don't get upset in there. Be careful," warned Cindy.

"If JayCee is in there, I'll just politely escort him out without causing a scene," said Jay.

Jay got out of the car, walked up to doors, and stood there for a long moment. A strange feeling ran down his back. As he entered the Poison Apple, the air gave him goose bumps. His hair on the back of his neck stood up on end. Jay looked around at the oddly dressed people, but he didn't see any sign of JayCee.

A young blonde waitress walked up to Jay. "Can I get you a table for you and your wife?"

It was really Bee, under the influence of her de-aging potion.

"Uh, no. I'm looking for someone," Jay said. "And how do you know if I'm married?"

"I'm clairvoyant. Besides, I saw your wedding ring. Your wife is sitting outside in the car when you came in," answered Bee.

"Do you know an Agnes Candlewick?" asked Jay.

"Sure I do. That's why we're crowded tonight with adult couples," said Bee.

"Agnes and Harriet, along with two friends plus three nice teenagers, all took the neighborhood children out to study the stars and have a campfire sleepover," said Bee, covering for Agnes who was setting up for the late night séance in the back room.

"So why don't you bring your lovely wife in and join the families in having an evening out," said Bee.

"No, I'll pass. I think I should just go home and get some sleep," said Jay as creepy and crawly mixed together and ran up his spine.

Bee and her two sisters showed up after their work was done in the tavern to finish the setup for the séance. Curtains had been drawn, candles were lit, and a large, round table was placed in the middle of the room. On the table sat a ruby crystalline amulet with an aura encircling it. Seven chairs circled the table.

Bee had Elizabeth on her right; Charmain was on her left. Agnes sat JayCee and Penelope across from Bee. Harriet was on Penelope's right. Agnes sat next to JayCee on his left.

Bee sat there with her eyes closed.

Elizabeth directed the séance, "Everyone place your hands on the table with your palms down. Touch your pinky fingers together."

JayCee heard a clock tower chime.

Charmain called out, "Who is the host of the amulet?"

A low voice spoke through Bee, "Benjamin Candlewick."

For some reason, JayCee caught himself as he counted the clock tower chimes in his head, "Five … six."

Charmain called out, "Who is the keeper of the amulet?"

The low voice answered again through Bee, "Agnes Candlewick."

JayCee counted the chimes, "Nine … ten"

Charmain called out, "Is the spirit of Benjamin Candlewick willing to communicate with Agnes Candlewick?"

JayCee heard the clock tower and counted in his head, "'Eleven … twelve."

On the twelfth chime, the air in the room thickened. The candle's flames stopped flickering. The temperature slowly dropped. JayCee could see everyone's breath was fogged except for Bee. The clock tower chimed a thirteenth time. JayCee wanted to ask why the clock tower chimed thirteen times, but he didn't say a word.

Bee's eyes opened. They glowed with ruby red flame in them.

"I enjoyed rocking on the porch with you, Agnes."

The voice was distant and echoed.

Agnes, who kept herself from crying and breaking the circle, answered back, "I am glad for that time together, Grandpa."

Charmain called out, "Agnes needs advice from beyond. Can you give her that advice?"

The distant echoed voice of Benjamin Candlewick came through Bee. Her eyes glowed with fire. "The one you seek is still alive. Look for his invisible journal. But beware of the warlock, for he looks to the boy as his way to return from the end of time."

The ruby red flames in Bee's eyes glowed brighter during this warning.

Benjamin continued, "Harriet, look under the porch for the—"

Bee's eyes faded as the voice faded away. The candles flickered again while the temperature in the room warmed up.

Elizabeth said, "Do not break the circle yet."

Charmain called out, "Another presence is here to speak to us."

Bee sat with her eyes closed. She was still in a trance, and she didn't move. A translucent black figure surrounded JayCee. His eyes rolled back in their sockets, making them completely white. The voice that came from JayCee was strong and deep.

"Sēo āne on āenigum tō forstoppian mē, tō lāc se cnapa on se Wīgbedd fram Blod!"

With horror in her face, Penelope let out a bloodcurdling scream. She broke the circle when she placed her hands over her mouth. Penelope shook, fearing the black magic sorcerer was going to forever possess JayCee.

"The voice did not come from the spirit world," said Elizabeth.

JayCee now sat limp in his chair with his head down into his chest. Harriet stared at both JayCee and Penelope.

She said, "What was that he was speaking?"

Penelope lowered her hands from her mouth and answered, "He was speaking Old English."

Agnes said, "It's obvious you understood what he said then."

Penelope, who was still shaking a little, translated, "He said, 'Sēo āne on āenigum', the only way, 'tō forstoppian mē', to stop me, 'tō lāc se cnapa', [is] to sacrifice the boy, 'on se Wīgbedd fram Blod!', on the Altar of Blood!"

Agnes picked up the amulet and stashed it in her pocket. "Penelope, rub JayCee's forehead with pixie dust."

Harriet said, "Better get a cauldron."

Penelope rubbed JayCee's forehead and the back of his neck with pixie dust. Her hands still shook, and her eyes blurred with tears. JayCee stirred to consciousness. As Harriet predicted, he needed a cauldron to vomit in.

Back at the Hidden Quiddity, Agnes sent Penelope off to bed.

"JayCee, you take my room," said Agnes.

Harriet started walking to her bedroom.

Agnes said, "Not you. We need to make a game plan."

The next morning, Jay had gotten up early for a Saturday. He went outside to get the newspaper and walk around the yard. It had been too dark the night before to see if JayCee had really worked on it. The hedges were trimmed perfectly. The lawn, both front and back, was manicured. Even the trees were shaped evenly.

"I know JayCee didn't do this," Jay thought.

Jay walked back toward the front porch, having bewildered and deranged thoughts of the events of the last twenty-four hours. Out of nowhere, Agnes, Harriet, Penelope, and JayCee appeared behind Jay's back.

"Good morning," said Agnes.

Jay quickly turned around, surprised. He felt the same way that he had at the Poison Apple the night before.

"Hi, Dad," said JayCee. Then he noticed the extremely manicured yard.

"Oh, no, I'm dead," JayCee thought.

Cindy called from the house, "Jay, can you come into the house?"

With the others following, Jay walked up the path to the entrance of the house. They found Cindy standing in the living room.

"Look, the wood floors are waxed and buffed. All the woodwork is polished. The whole house is immaculate. Even the counter appliances in the kitchen are sparkling clean," said Cindy, astonished.

Agnes turned to Harriet and whispered, "Only the yard, Harriet."

"You know those gnomes. They're clean freaks," whispered Harriet.

Both Jay and Cindy turned to Agnes, feeling puzzled and shocked.

Agnes, trying not to look uneasy, asked, "We would like to ask a favor. Would you allow Penelope to stay with you this next week? Harriet and I have to go out of town to purchase merchandise and take care of a legal matter."

Cindy spoke first, knowing she had been waiting for an opportunity like this to find out more about this odd little girl from England.

Cindy said, "We would love to have Penelope stay with us."

Jay just stood there as creepy and crawly ran up his spine. He said nothing about the yard work, the clean house, and what Agnes had asked.

"Shall I make breakfast for all of us?" said Cindy.

And off she went into the sparkling kitchen.

Chapter Twenty
What's Under the Porch?

That next week, Penelope stayed in the Münter's guest room. Agnes and Harriet traveled to their grandfather's farm that now belonged to their parents. Ma and Pa Candlewick had been sitting on the porch and rocking quietly when Agnes and Harriet appeared.

"Look, Pa, it's Agnes and Harriet," said Ma.

"I'll start some water for tea, Ma," said Pa.

Agnes and Harriet came up to the porch and hugged their mother.

"What brings you out to the straw farm?" asked Ma.

"We had a séance and made contact with Grandpa," said Harriet. "And he told me to look under the porch."

"Look under the porch for what?" asked Pa, coming outside with cups of tea and crackers.

"We don't know," said Agnes.

She gave them the details of the séance.

After the tea and crackers, Pa crawled under the porch, holding onto a magic torch that lit the way. The magic torch suddenly acted like a divining rod. It turned right and then left. Then it wiggled up and then down as Pa crawled further back under the porch. The torch brightened its glow as it guided him to a spot at the back of the porch next to the foundation.

"Toss me a hand shovel," Pa called out.

He dug around until he finally uncovered a strongbox. Pa pulled the box out with him as he inched back out. Up on the porch, he cleaned off the box.

"There appears no way to open it. Well, Harriet, this is your secret to unravel," said Pa.

Harriet looked the box over. There were no hinges, a hasp, or even seams.

She tried tapping the box with her wand and said, "Open, open, open." She even tried an old cliché. "Open sesame."

Then Agnes said, "What about the story Grandpa would tell us about the best things in life are hidden from us and are never solid or concrete."

Harriet stared at the metal box. "I know what is inside."

She placed her hands on the sides of the box. She thought of the times she spent with her grandmother.

"Oh, how I loved the potions and charms Grandma conjured up. I told her I wished I had her power to do what she could do," explained Harriet.

The top of the box folded open. Inside was exactly what Harriet had imagined.

"It's Grandma's amulet and her wand. To Grandpa, she was the best thing in his life. Thank you, Grandpa," said Harriet. Tears formed in her eyes.

During the week Penelope was at the Münter's house, she tried to keep from saying or doing anything that Cindy would have found unusual or strange. Sunshine kept herself hidden behind Penelope's left ear, except for when she flew out to the garden to eat pollen and drink nectar from the flowers. Penelope helped Cindy in the kitchen, even though she had no idea what a lot of the things did in there.

Cindy asked, "Penelope, can you help me unload the dishwasher?"

Penelope remembered something from when she was there for dinner. JayCee had put the dishes into a box with pullout racks. Penelope pulled open the dishwasher door and looked inside.

Cindy wasn't in the kitchen, so Penelope pulled out her wand, pointed it at the dishes, and said, "Put away."

The dishes, pans, and flatware spun out of the dishwasher and flew to their respective places of storage. It was a bit noisy in the kitchen. The plates clattered, the pans clanged together, and the flatware hit the drawer like machine gun fire. Hearing all the noise, Cindy ran into the kitchen and saw Penelope standing there with one dirty plate in her right hand as she set it in the lower rack of the dishwasher.

Shocked, Cindy looked around the kitchen. She expected to see a mess of broken dishes. Cindy changed her facial expression from a bewildered look to a smile but failed miserably.

"Thank you, Penelope. I'll load the dirty dishes after dinner tonight," said Cindy.

Penelope went outside to where JayCee had been working around the yard. Nothing really needed to be done since the gnomes kept up the yard and the fairies that had moved into the garden kept away the weeds.

"I have wanted to talk to you alone for quite some time. There are things I need to tell you," said Penelope, worriedly.

They sat under the large tree that JayCee now thought of as their tree.

JayCee said, "I didn't understand all that has been going on, but I have a better understanding now."

Penelope took hold of JayCee's hand and looked at him with her majestic green eyes.

She said, "When Agnes first told me that I was your one true love, I thought she was playing a joke on me. Especially with the part that I was keeping you from falling toward black magic, I wasn't really sure how you were connected to any magic at all."

Penelope's words transfixed JayCee.

She continued, "But you don't know that, after you looked into the scrying mirror and after we had the séance, Agnes had me rub your forehead and neck with pixie dust to make you feel better."

JayCee tried to speak, but Penelope put a finger up to his mouth.

"I think those are the times you were most vulnerable to the black magic. That was when I kept you from going there," continued Penelope. She unintentionally rubbed JayCee's face and neck. "You must have felt my magical energy pulling you back to me." She placed her forehead against JayCee's own forehead.

Penelope admitted frankly, "What Agnes and Harriet couldn't tell me was if you are my one true love. I promised myself that I would love you anyway and try to keep you from going over to black magic."

Penelope pulled back from JayCee after realizing her emotions were showing too much.

With a small tear in her eye, she continued, "When Sunshine brought you to me and had you rub my face with pixie dust, it was then I knew you were my one true love only because Sunshine has never given anyone else pixie dust except to me."

"I know we are only thirteen years old and not really old enough for all of this," said Penelope. She lifted up her head to get control of herself. "When summer is over, I have to go home. I just wanted you to know that, when we do grow up, I would like to try again. That is, if we grow up." She gave JayCee a half-smile.

JayCee began to say something, but Penelope cut him off. "There's one more thing. At the séance, Oozar the Sorcerer spoke through you. He said the only way to stop him was to sacrifice you on the Altar of Blood."

Penelope thought, "I've said too much."

JayCee blurted out, "The Altar of Blood? That sounds gruesome."

"Oh, it is," said Penelope. "To wizards and witches, this is the most horrifying death ritual."

"You said sacrifice. To whom is one sacrificed?" asked JayCee.

"Not to anyone. It's to what they are sacrificed for," answered Penelope. "It is to stop black magic from overpowering white magic and keep magical powers balanced in the universe." She had a stern look on her face.

"How will sacrificing me stop this Oozar guy?" asked JayCee worriedly.

"By eliminating you, he cannot posses you, so he can't return and use his powerful black magic to gain control over the magical and nonmagical world," answered Penelope.

"A wizard named McDermit gives me the black magic power from a sorcerer," said JayCee. "Harriet gets me to love you with a magic potion so Agnes can entrap me into this magical world through a séance." He paused to collect his thoughts and pulled his hand away from Penelope's. "So now the three of you can to sacrifice me in a death ritual on a witch's altar to stop Oozar from possessing me to keep the two magical powers in balance? Is that what this is all about?"

JayCee was more worried about what was to come next as he looked into Penelope's hypnotic green eyes.

"No," said Penelope sternly. "I love you. I won't let you be sacrificed or become possessed by a sorcerer. Please, JayCee, you must believe that Agnes and Harriet are doing the best they can to stop all of this from happening." Penelope again grabbed JayCee's hand. Pure emotion showed in her face and eyes. "Also, you and I are in love with each other because we were meant to be. You and I were to meet and fall in love no matter what, according to an alternate timeline trance I did."

JayCee looked at Penelope, perplexed at what she had just said.

"Whether you had magical powers or not, we were meant to be together," affirmed Penelope.

"Can you see our future?" asked JayCee, astonished.

"The alternate timeline trance can only show up to the present time, just in a different way," Penelope said. "We still meet at the Renaissance Faire. But you do not have any magical powers. It was by pure chance that you stopped at the booth and we started talking without any prompting from Harriet or love potions. The one difference was that yesterday would have been the day I told you that I'm a witch. I don't know what that would have done to our relationship. Again, that was an alternative timeline, and that outcome doesn't matter now."

Both JayCee and Penelope sat there quietly as they held each other's hands.

Unbeknownst to JayCee and Penelope, Cindy had been at the kitchen window the whole time and listened to their conversation.

"I knew Penelope was a strange little girl in an eerie way. Playing a child's game of being a witch is one thing, but this talk of blood sacrifice has gone too far," said Cindy aloud. "And those two sisters talking of true love to impressionable, young adolescent kids. I'll have some words to tell them when they get back." Her temper rose.

She had a disturbing thought, "What about all this talk of witchcraft and magic?"

Cindy thought about the past couple days, including the odd behavior of everyone at that children's party and the eerie-looking tavern with the flaming sign.

"And what of the pristine yard work and the sparkling kitchen?" Cindy thought nervously.

Cindy gasped and spoke aloud, "Penelope and her cousins are witches."

Cindy's blood began to boil with anger and outrage.

"I will put a stop to this magical love affair before it goes too much farther," said Cindy.

Sunshine had her own problems to deal with. She was in the garden eating pollen and drinking nectar when two fairies grabbed her.

"Who said you could eat in our garden, pixie?" said one of the fairies.

"We finally caught you," said the other fairy.

The two fairies threw Sunshine into a spiderweb of an orb spider. One of the many differences between pixies and fairies is that pixies spend quite a bit of time studying magic. Even though they don't take it very seriously, it does come in handy at times.

Sunshine pulled out her little wand made from a hornet's stinger and sent the Snarf curse at the two fairies. Both fairies dropped to the ground, now in a deep coma.

Then Sunshine turned to the spider, stared at its eyes, and pointed her wand at her. The spider backed up to the farthest part of the web and stayed there. Sunshine's wings were stuck to the sticky part of the web, and she couldn't get them to move or break free. Sunshine dared not cut the web because she would fall to the ground and still not be able to fly.

JayCee and Penelope walked around the house holding hands. As they passed the garden, JayCee noticed Sunshine stuck in a spiderweb.

"Penelope, isn't that Sunshine right there?" asked JayCee, pointing at the web.

"Oh, Sunshine!" said Penelope.

Penelope pulled out her wand and touched Sunshine on her wings. Sunshine was released from the web. She flew up to Penelope and hid behind her left ear.

"How do you think she got caught in the spiderweb?" asked JayCee.

"Look down there at the two fairies on the ground. They must have caught Sunshine in the garden. Fairies are very territorial. Also, they do not like pixies," said Penelope.

"Are they dead?" asked JayCee.

"No, Sunshine probably cursed them to sleep for a long time," said Penelope. "They will wake up and go about their business of tending the garden."

At that same moment, Cindy made her move after a long thought on the matter of what to do about Penelope. She went out on the front porch and called out to Penelope with a slight change to her voice and attitude.

"Penelope, could you help me with making dinner?" she asked.

Chapter Twenty-one
Which Witch Is a
Witch or Not

When Agnes returned to Broomstick, she went to the Poison Apple and talked with Bee.

"Where did Franklin live?" asked Agnes.

"Here, as far as I know," said Bee, laughing.

The tavern keep came over to Agnes. "I know where he lived before he disappeared. He told me once that he had a place at the factory because it had the best security for what he was working on."

"Do you know what Franklin was doing that he needed security for?" asked Agnes.

"He only talked about one thing. You," said the tavern keep.

"He would talk to you about me?" asked Agnes.

"It was more like he would ask about you. How you are doing with the potion shop? If you were interested in anyone?" said the tavern keep.

When Agnes went to pick up Penelope at the Münter's house, she was greeted with more than she expected. Jay wasn't home from work just yet, and Cindy was in a strange mood, as if she knew a secret and wanted to tell the whole world.

"Having Penelope here this last week was educational to say the least," said Cindy. "She is a delightful girl and very helpful around the house. You might even say we made a magical connection."

Agnes smiled and acted as if she didn't know what the implication of the statement meant.

She said, "Harriet and I really thank you for taking care of Penelope this week."

"Cousin Agnes, we really should be going. Mr. Münter will be coming home soon for supper," said Penelope, feeling a little concerned.

"My dad just pulled up," said JayCee worriedly.

"That's good. Because I need to ask Jay an important question," said Agnes.

"Can it wait until tomorrow, Cousin Agnes?" asked Penelope with a little more urgency in her tone.

Jay opened the door and walked into the living room.

"Good evening, all," said Jay. His smile seemed to be pasted on his face by something other than normal circumstances.

Agnes noticed Jay was happier than his normal self.

She said, "I would like to thank you and Cindy again for taking care of Penelope this week. I do need to ask you a question before we leave and let you get back to your normal routine."

"Ask away," said Jay happily.

"That evening, when you came to pick up JayCee, Robert Brown came over. He was arguing with you about something you didn't understand at work, and it involved knowing his neighbors," said Agnes.

Jay explained about the budget reports from a division where Robert was recently promoted to being the production manager. He told Agnes about Robert's excuses involving a Mr. Stiltskins and a Mr. Nymph for inadequate numbers by not giving him a correct straw-to-gold ratio. Jay also spoke of the missing name of the hand-braided rope manufacturer.

He said, "He tells me it's a government contract, and I needed a top-secret clearance. So he was telling me nonsense to cover up his recordkeeping errors."

Jay stopped his griping and went back to smiling at Agnes.

"I can fix your problem with Mr. Brown," said Agnes. "Again, thank you for this week."

Agnes and Penelope headed for the door as JayCee walked behind them.

Just outside, JayCee asked Penelope, "How long will this last?"

"How long will what last?" asked Agnes.

"A couple more days, and then it will all wear off," answered Penelope.

"What will wear off?" asked Agnes.

"Can I explain this when we get home?" urged Penelope.

Agnes sent Penelope home to the Hidden Quiddity and went over to Robert Brown's house. Agnes rang the doorbell. Since the time when Jay had barged in, Robert had installed a chain lock and a peephole on the front door.

Robert called through the door, "What do you want?"

"You have a bookkeeping problem," said Agnes.

"That's none of your business," stated Robert.

"You're right. That's none of my business. But my business is inside the living quarters of Franklin McDermit. We can help each other," stated Agnes. "Open the door, and let's talk face to face. Or I could just pop in."

"No, no. I'll open the door," said Robert, opening the door.

Agnes said, "Let's go into your kitchen and make some tea."

In the kitchen, Robert filled the kettle with water.

"What do you know about my bookkeeping problem?" asked Robert.

"For thirteen years, the books have been doing themselves. Because of your appointment, the books are jealous. They must feel they are not doing a good job. You, on the other hand, are trying to figure out the reports. You are making a mess of it because you do not understand the magical world. How am I doing?" said Agnes.

"Those books bit me and sprayed red ink at my shirt the first time I opened them. Accounting was outdated. So I tried to computerize the recordkeeping reports. And all those—" Robert paused. "Those creatures who can account for them on a payroll if you don't know how or what they are paid," said Robert.

"I can fix your problem. You will have to hire me as your personal assistant with full access to the entire production building and unlimited authority over all personnel," said Agnes, laying out her proposal to Robert.

"So what is your business in the living quarters?" asked Robert.

"Do you really want to know?" asked Agnes.

Robert demanded, "And what do I get out of all of this?

"For starters, the books won't get even angrier," Agnes countered.

Then she added for good measure, "Surely you realize that biting and shooting ink are only the beginning. Still want to know what my business is in the living quarters?"

"Uh, no, I don't think so," answered Robert.

Agnes went back to the Hidden Quiddity and found Penelope and Harriet sitting in the reading room where the crystal ball sat on the small table.

"We have corrupted this nice little girl," said Harriet.

"Would you like to tell me what happened at the Münter's house this week?" asked Agnes.

Penelope explained she told JayCee her side of everything that had been going on. She said Cindy had listened in at the kitchen window and heard every word.

"Cindy called me into the kitchen to help with making dinner. At first, she acted like everything was all right. Then Cindy asked me about my feeling toward JayCee. I told her that I liked him very much. He was fun to be with," said Penelope. "Cindy came out and said she overheard us talking. She wanted to know why a little witch like me had to prey upon JayCee's emotions. I was taken aback, and I had no answer to give her. I tried to explain that being a witch wasn't a bad thing. I wasn't preying upon JayCee's emotions for any magical gain."

Penelope continued, "During cooking, Cindy started to pull out the bay leaves. Then she said an awful thing to me. From now on, we would be using the silverware. I just had to do something to protect both JayCee and myself."

"So what did you do?" questioned Agnes.

"I used my wand to replace the bay leaves with hazelnut leaves. I added pixie dust to the salt and pepper shakers and charmed the house to make Cindy and Jay not do anything unless I allowed it. It's only temporary. But, when it wears off in a couple days, Cindy will remember everything. That is what I am really worried about," explained Penelope.

"Everything will be all right, Penelope. We have two days before we have to do anything about it," said Agnes. She turned to Harriet. "I talked to Robert Brown, and he said Franklin had living quarters at the plant. I offered to fix his record book problem to get access in."

"I'll stick a wand in his side and threaten to turn him into a toad if he doesn't let us in," said Harriet.

"No, let's not do that," said Agnes.

"How about offering Mr. Brown three wishes?" asked Penelope.

"You know witches don't grant wishes," said Harriet. "I'll threaten to turn his son into a skunk."

"I know we don't do wishes. But he does," said Penelope, pointing at the old lamp on the top shelf.

"How do you know that lamp has a genie in it?" asked Agnes.

"You had me clean off all the shelves. I polished it to make it look nice," said Penelope.

"You didn't wish for anything, did you?" Agnes asked, alarmed.

"Oh, no," said Penelope, smiling. "After I told him my name, he asked if I was related to a wizard from centuries ago. After I thought about it and answered yes, his color turned a grizzly pale color as if he were about to get sick. After that, we were good friends. He has been very polite since."

"I still want to scare Robert Brown into letting us into McDermit's private quarters," said Harriet, smirking.

Agnes just said, "We'll see if Robert Brown takes my proposal, hires me, and gives me full access before we go to any unusual diplomacy."

When Agnes went over to see Cindy two days later, she found a series of large nails stuck in the grass and dirt of the front yard. On the door was a wreath made of branches of the laurel tree. In the big bay window hung a suncatcher made of colored glass balls.

Agnes walked up to the door and rang the doorbell. Cindy opened the door part of the way. Cindy was standing there with bay leaves tied around her neck.

"Aren't you overdoing this, Cindy?" said Agnes. "In a sense, you are doing witchcraft with the nails in the footprint spell, the laurel tree wreath, the bay leaf charms, and the window decoration house enchantment. Now who's the witch?" asked Agnes.

"I'm not the witch. You are. And your little cousin, too," said Cindy in a defensive voice.

"What did Penelope do to make you want to harm her?" asked Agnes.

"I don't want to harm her. I just want her and you to stay away from my son," said Cindy.

"You knew that using silverware and putting bay leaves in the food would cause harm to Penelope, and you were going to do that," said Agnes.

"I was just—"

Agnes interrupted, "What does that say about you, Cindy?"

"I never meant—"

Agnes jumped in again, "So who is the harmful person here? You or us?"

"But you—"

"Do you realize you also are endangering your own son with all this anti-witch magic you are doing?" continued Agnes.

"JayCee isn't—" said Cindy.

"After all, as you now know, he is connected by black magic to a wizard, making him vulnerable, like Penelope, to your harmful actions. These are thirteen-year-old kids, Cindy," concluded Agnes. "Now why don't we sit down and have some coffee and tea. I'll tell you everything that is going on and what I am doing about it." Agnes had kindness in her voice. "First, would you please remove the bay leaves from around your neck? It's a little annoying."

Cindy opened the door and allowed Agnes into the house. JayCee had been at the top of the stairs. He had been listening to what was going on. He hadn't seen or heard from Penelope those last two days. The front of the house gave him an eerie feeling, and he didn't venture near it. Even the gnomes had stopped taking care of the lawn and flowerbeds.

Cindy took off the bay leaves and set them on the kitchen counter near the spice rack.

"I was scared," said Cindy as a mild defense.

"So was Penelope," stated Agnes. "Bay leaves are a minor annoyance. It only makes us feel ill, but silver is poison.

"All I wanted to do was to stop her witchcraft-induced love control over JayCee," said Cindy.

JayCee came into the kitchen. "Penelope doesn't have any control over me. I fell in love with her all on my own. Penelope being a witch made me more attracted to her. She understood what I have been going through. You and Dad wouldn't even listen to me when I tried to tell you something was making me do unusual things."

"JayCee, go and see Penelope. Just think to yourself 'Hidden Quiddity,'" said Agnes.

JayCee closed his eyes and thought, "Hidden Quiddity."

Right in front of Cindy's eyes, JayCee disappeared in a puff of apple green smoke.

"Let them have their summer love," said Agnes. "Now, as to what is happening."

Agnes removed all memory charms from Cindy and proceeded to fill in the rest of the information.

When JayCee appeared in the Hidden Quiddity, Penelope came from behind the counter and hugged him.

"I thought I wouldn't be able to see you again, and you might be in danger," said Penelope, holding JayCee like she would never let him go.

"Mom got a little weird. She looked for any footprints in the front yard and drove nail spikes into them. On our front door is a laurel tree branch wreath. She has been wearing bay leaves around her neck. Can we go over to the Poison Apple? I've been eating out of the garden, avoiding any food she made," explained JayCee.

"Harriet's not here, so I can't leave. I do know how to make some things to eat if you're willing to try it," said Penelope, all excited about her chance at magical cooking.

Not everything came out perfect. The spider legs were slightly burnt, and the chocolate cake fell on one side. But JayCee didn't notice. To him, it all tasted great.

One of the signs of true love was when her bad cooking tasted better than his mother's good cooking.

Harriet came back in a frisky mood with a mischievous smile on her face. She was surprised to see JayCee at the potion shop. When Harriet walked into the back area of the shop, Penelope and JayCee suddenly stopped hugging each other.

"You have chocolate cake on your face, JayCee," said Harriet.

JayCee explained what the last two days were like. His mom had done strange stuff that supposedly kept witches away.

"I never felt so uncomfortable like that before," expressed JayCee.

When Agnes returned from talking to Cindy, she told JayCee all the charms and enchantments to expel witches were removed.

She said, "It's safe to go back home. Your mom knows the whole story. There are no more memory charms on her. She promised not to tell your dad any of this because of how he might react. This may be a good time to talk to your mom about how you feel with all this."

The day after Agnes talked to Robert Brown, he went in to see H.G. White.

"I need an assistant. Someone who can help me with the reports," said Robert.

H.G. White looked at Robert. "Do you have someone in mind?"

"Yes, I do. She's a … She's a …" Robert stuttered.

"Well, go on. Say it," prompted H.G. White.

"She's a witch," said Robert.

H.G. White felt a chill that ran down his back. He said, "Ah. Do what you feel you need to do, Robert."

In the human resources office, Robert filled out the form with the title of "Top Executive Assistant to the Production Manager of the Broomstick Division (Unrestricted Access)."

"Mr. White will have to approve this himself," said the human resources manager.

Before Robert had the slightest chance to stop the manager, she was out of the office and heading down the hall. A few minutes later, she returned from Mr. White's office, frazzled.

"Uh, he said you can sign it," she said.

When Agnes showed up at Robert's office, he pointed to the bottom left-hand drawer of his desk.

"They're in there," said Robert.

Agnes opened the drawer. "I'm here to help you."

She reached into the drawer and pulled out the two record books. They snarled at her as she set them on the desk.

Agnes pulled out her wand, pointed at them, and said, "If you misbehave, I'll dump you right in the shredding machine and then reglue you back together to do it again." Agnes looked up at Robert. "Maybe I should do this alone."

"You know, I'll just step down to the cafeteria," said Robert, befuddled at the sight.

"If I do this, you really won't have a job," stated Agnes.

"That's okay. I can find something else to occupy my workday," said Robert, backing out of his office.

Chapter Twenty-two
Finding McDermit's
Hidden Journal

The two record books were old leather ledgers that had kept track of the production line from the very first day and the first broom made. The coarse brown leather was well-weathered, and the yellowed pages were rounded at the corners. The first record book was labeled "broomsticks." The second record book had "pay records" on the front.

As the books sat on the desk, they snarled and spit to show they were upset with the situation. Agnes began by calming them down with some fresh lemon oil for the leather covers. Then she went to work.

"First, do you know where McDermit's journal is?" asked Agnes.

The broom book gurgled at Agnes, fluttering its pages at her.

"What do you mean? Which volume?" retorted Agnes angrily. "How about all of them, including the last one he was working on?"

Robert was sitting alone at a table in the cafeteria drinking coffee when Jay came over.

"Mind if I sit down?" asked Jay.

Robert motioned toward a chair.

"I just want to smooth things out," said Jay. "Agnes Candlewick asked about the problem between us. I told her about your recordkeeping and the nonsense answers you gave me."

Robert waved his hand at Jay, indicating for him to lower his voice. "This is not the place to discuss any of this."

"Now wait, Robert. She had a look on her face that told me she understood everything I was saying. Then she said she could fix it," said Jay in a low voice.

Sipping his coffee, Robert said, "She came to see me and told me exactly what my problem was without me telling her anything. She offered to fix it if I hired her and gave her unrestricted access to the production building. She is up in my office now, looking over the records."

"Why is she allowed to see your records and not me, the chief financial officer?" asked Jay.

"Because she is one of them," whispered Robert.

"You've said that before. What do you mean by one of them and those people?" questioned Jay.

"Listen, I can't tell you. But that's why I sent you to the Poison Apple to find out for yourself. Then it was up to you to decide what you wanted to do with the information," said Robert.

Agnes, who stood next to the table, appeared unexpectedly from out of nowhere, interrupting their discussion. Jay sat there, giving a turn as to what just took place. Agnes cleared her throat to get their attention.

"Excuse me," said Agnes. "I found the errors in the records. A copy of the report is on your desk, and it is being processed into the data bank, Mr. Münter."

"Ah, I gotta go," said Robert.

"Now can you take me over to McDermit's quarters," said Agnes.

"Right this way, Miss Candlewick," said Robert.

The two of them went over to the broomstick manufacturing building. From the observation platform, Agnes saw everything.

She turned to Robert. "How did you get trapped into this in the first place?"

"I recognized some of my neighbors as working over here. Then Mr. White gave me the promotion without really telling me about this until after I signed the waver. Then it was too late. He had Winston Wisestone show me this factory, and he told me what would happen to me if I told anyone, including my family," explained Robert.

"You're his scapegoat," said Agnes. "I can fix that, too."

"No, please, I like my job. I mean how much I'm being paid, that is," pleaded Robert. "Over here is McDermit's office. It's where I found the record books."

Once inside, Agnes was allowed access into Franklin's living quarters. Robert never could get the door open.

"Hey, I got to get back to my office," said Robert nervously.

"Why don't you take the day off and take your wife shopping? You know a company party is coming up. It's a big social event that Edna wouldn't want to miss," suggested Agnes.

Robert quietly gestured at Agnes with his two index fingers and stepped out of Franklin's living quarters.

In one of the rooms, the walls were filled with books. The record books were right about volumes. On one wall were Franklin's private journals.

In the middle of the room was a stone slab table. On it was what looked like Franklin's last journal he had been working in. Next to it was an Old English dictionary, papers scribbled on, an inkwell, and quills. All of this had thirteen years of dust that covered it. At the other end of the table was a U.S. Geological Survey map. Circled on the map was an entrance to a cavern.

"That's it," said Agnes aloud. She gathered up the map, the journal, the Old English dictionary, and the scribbled papers.

Agnes had just started out the door when an odd little man met her. The stiltskin stood there, not allowing Agnes to pass.

"I'm sorry, missy, but yer not to remove those items from here," said the stiltskin.

"Do you know who I am?" demanded Agnes.

"Yes, I do. Yer the new top executive assistant to that production manager," said the little man.

"That's right, and I have full access to this plant," Agnes said, continuing to be annoyed.

"That may be so, missy. But those are Mr. McDermit's personal belongings. Them's his orders. Nothing is to leave here," said the stiltskin.

"McDermit has not been here for thirteen years. These are now company records, and you work for me now," stated Agnes, poking at the little man. "And, if you don't get out of my way, I'll have you spinning straw into gold for every little girl in the world that has even been called 'princess.'"

"Beggin' your pardon, missy," said the little man.

"Miss Candlewick to you," said Agnes. She stormed away, actually feeling good about herself.

"Hawkins, my name," said the stiltskin under his breath.

Robert checked the company calendar, and Agnes was right. A company party was coming up. Robert went home and convinced Edna to go shopping.

"Spend as much as you want, Edna," said Robert. "This will be a big social event since I'm a production manager."

"What about them? Will they be there?" asked Edna.

Robert explained, "We are in the elite status with my job. We know who is and who isn't. There are people above me who do not even know of them. And, if you want to stay in this elite class, Edna, you don't want to tell those who don't know anything about them."

We are special, aren't we, Robert?" said Edna with a certain air about her.

JayCee and Penelope spent the day with JayCee's friends. They went to a pizza parlor for lunch. Penelope enjoyed being in the nonmagical world because it was so different. But JayCee would have rather talked about Penelope's world of magic. He wished he could be a real wizard. Since he found out that he wasn't even a wizard's apprentice, just a pawn caught up in a terrible struggle between two wizards, he had felt not worthy to even be with Penelope.

"I'm in love with a witch, and I can't do simple magic without it causing problems for everyone," thought JayCee.

As JayCee sat there, he felt a cold depression had taken control of his thoughts, like he needed to do something. The task was unclear, fuzzy in his mind. He concentrated to make it clear.

"JayCee, what's wrong?" Penelope asked, sitting next to him. She held his limp body.

JayCee's nonmagical friends stared at him. "What's wrong with JayCee?"

An employee of the pizza parlor rushed over. "I called for the paramedics."

Two other patrons came over, pulled JayCee away from Penelope, and laid him on the floor.

"His breathing is slow, and his heart rate is forty-five," said one person.

The other person pulled a tablecloth off a table and used it to cover JayCee. Penelope knew what she should have done, but they were in a place filled with nonmagical people. In the background, she heard a sound like someone was tormenting an old dog. The sound was getting louder. Outside, a red-paneled truck pulled up. Two men in white outfits jump out. They carried black boxes and headed straight for where JayCee was laying on the floor.

Penelope watched in fear. She wished she had just grabbed JayCee and went to Agnes. One of the men wrapped something around JayCee's arm and pumped it up. The other man held a metal cylinder that emitted light. He opened JayCee's eyes and shined it into them.

"BP ninety over sixty-five. Breathing is slow, but steady at twelve. Did anyone see this boy take anything?" asked one of the paramedics.

Two men in black outfits came in. They talked to the employee and one of the paramedics. The employee pointed over to Penelope and JayCee's friends. The two men walked over to them.

"Empty your pockets on the table," said one of the men wearing black. A metal crest was on the left side of his shirt.

JayCee's friends complied quickly. They had gum and wrappers, paper money and change, a pen, and ticket stubs from a movie.

"And you too, miss," said the man.

All Penelope had on her was her magic wand.

"What's this?" asked the police officer.

"My magic wand," said Penelope.

The paramedics put JayCee on a stretcher and rolled him out to the ambulance.

Very upset, Penelope said, "I need to go with him."

"Are you his sister?" asked the officer.

"No, I'm … his cousin visiting from England, and I know how to reach his parents," Penelope said as she tried to stay with JayCee.

Penelope asked, "Can I have my magic wand back?"

When Agnes got back to the Hidden Quiddity, she told Harriet about the little man.

"Oh, I don't like stiltskins," said Harriet. "I would have turned him into a small bug and stepped on him."

Agnes laid out the U.S. Geological Survey map. "We need to find this cavern. That's where McDermit might have been when I saw him in the crystal ball." She continued to describe the events of the day. "And there in his study was this stone table."

When Agnes was ten years old, she received the crystal ball with golden legs of dragon talons as a birthday present from her grandfather. She would stare into the ball while trying to see the future. One day at a quarter past two in the afternoon, she saw herself and Franklin in front of a stone slab table. He was weak, and she was holding him up. They were older in the crystal ball though. She knew they had a connection. When she saw Franklin, Agnes told him of the crystal ball and what she saw. Franklin was, however, twenty years old.

"Please, Agnes," said Franklin. "You're a very sweet girl. But I'm too old for you."

He didn't really want to say she was too young. Agnes knew that is what he meant. She still grew up with feelings in her heart for him.

In her ear, Agnes heard the magical telephone that rang when Cindy would call.

"Hello, Cindy," said Agnes. She paused. A worried expression came over her face. "In a coma?" She paused again. Agnes then used a more reassuring voice. "No, it is not your fault. I'll be right there."

Agnes turned to Harriet. "JayCee is in trouble. We need to get to Broomstick Hospital's emergency room before they do something to him."

Both Agnes and Harriet disappeared and showed up at the emergency room, where they found Penelope and Cindy together. Penelope told Agnes what had happened at the pizza parlor and how there were too many people for her to do anything.

Agnes and Harriet disappeared from the waiting room and reappeared in the curtained area of the emergency room where JayCee was. Agnes and Harriet grabbed hold of the bed frame and chanted a short phrase.

"Counter Pluotes."

The area turned black with only a dim light around the three of them. The curtain was drawn back, and magical medical staff in white robes and pointed brim hats came in around the bed.

"Definitely latter stages of spiritualistical possession compounded by fluctuation of the controlling continuum," said the witch doctor. "Rest and time, the full possession will be complete," recommended the witch doctor.

"That is not what we want," said Agnes. "He was about to be treated on the other side by nonmagical medical doctors. I needed to get him out of there. If you will allow me, I can take care of this and be out of your way in ten minutes." Urgency was in her voice.

"Well, if you want to play witch doctor, go right ahead," said the emergency room witch doctor as he walked away.

Harriet went back to the waiting room of the regular hospital. She retrieved Penelope and brought Cindy over to the magical side of the hospital where her and Agnes transferred JayCee.

When Cindy arrived, she saw her son strapped down in the metal-framed bed with scorching red eyes. He was speaking incoherently as a blackened shadow circled around him. Agnes had Penelope rub pixie dust on JayCee's forehead. Cindy stood there and watched as JayCee came out of the trans-coma.

"I must go and bring back," JayCee mumbled. "Not clear enough yet."

"Each time we get another piece of this puzzle, JayCee has one of these," declared Agnes to Cindy.

"Maybe Oozar is getting desperate and trying harder to get JayCee to do what he needs done?" asked Harriet.

JayCee reached out to Penelope. She hugged JayCee tightly as the two of them cried. JayCee did not realize that his mother had been standing there. Cindy was completely numb.

Agnes brought JayCee and Cindy back home while Harriet and Penelope went back to the Hidden Quiddity. Cindy was completely insensible. She was overwhelmed with the situation of her world being turned inside, outside, and upside down. Agnes could not let her down easy anymore either.

"Now can we be friends, Cindy," said Agnes sympathetically.

"You want to still be my friend after what I tried to do and the resentment I showed toward you?" asked Cindy.

"Yes, Cindy, I still want to be friends with you," said Agnes.

Cindy hugged Agnes and began to cry. "I'm sorry for what I have done. Forgive me, Agnes."

When Agnes came home to the Hidden Quiddity, she asked Penelope to translate some Old English. Spread out on a table was McDermit's last journal he had written in, along with the scribbled notes and the Old English dictionary.

"The journal doesn't have any Old English or translations written in it," said Harriet as she turned the pages. "The last entry in the journal was about a woman in the South Pacific islands that used gemstones for healing. The villagers almost killed Franklin for exposing the woman as a fraud.

Penelope scanned through the scribbled notes. "These are Old English words. Funny though, don't you think the translation for the words would be written on here also? This one scribbled note is of Old English sentences while this other note is a list of things. This one sentence fragment 'blandan mihtig wyrtrumas' means 'mixing powerful roots.'"

"Are you sure about the translation of roots? Because the two items we know Franklin collected were not plant roots at all," said Agnes.

Penelope just shrugged her shoulders, not understanding the connection.

She said, "And this sentence at the top of this other list refers to 'Iseard,' which means 'Iceland.'" She read a list of words aloud in Old English. "Molten clud. Rēad aernemergen fram seō noro. Īs. Ācwelan waēpnedmanns blāēd."

Penelope looked up at Agnes and Harriet.

She asked, "What would these have to do with mixing up something? Molten rock, red dawn of the north, ice, and—" Penelope stumbled through the translation. "Die mans breathe. To die mans breath, possibly dying man's breath."

"Earth, fire, water, and air," said Agnes.

"But Franklin collected a newborn baby's breath," asked Penelope.

"So all we have is a map, a few translated words, and a journal with its last pages blank," said Harriet, not feeling very optimistic.

Agnes thought about it while she stared and touched the pages. "The inkwell and quills," said Agnes. "They're blank because Franklin wanted them hidden. Rub your hand across the page! Feel it?"

Both Harriet and Penelope rubbed the page. Some of the ink had dried. There were little bumps like the dots over the Is and other punctuation marks.

"I need to get the inkwell and quills off the table," said Agnes as she turned and disappeared.

Even though it was late at night, Agnes went to the broomstick building. The little man met her at the living quarters.

"Back again, missy?" said the stiltskin. "I mean, Miss Candlewick."

Agnes asked, "How long has Franklin had this table?"

"O, E, bout it when E's only twenty. E said it was a present to a pretty girl when she got older," answered the stiltskin.

Agnes became upset with that bit of news. She just grabbed the inkwell and quills and left.

Agnes took a little longer to get back to the Hidden Quiddity. She stopped by the town's cemetery where it was peaceful, quiet, and dark. She wanted to be alone with her thoughts. All her emotions swirled around in her head. Anger, torment, and resentment were the strongest until Agnes settled on the one real emotion that she kept hidden deep inside her.

"You've been crying, Agnes," said Harriet.

"He bought that table after I told him what I saw in the crystal ball, about us being in love and everything. He was waiting for me to grow up," explained Agnes.

Harriet knew it was better to change the subject, so she asked, "So what are you going to do with the ink?"

Agnes poured a little ink on a cloth and rubbed the blank page with it. As she rubbed in the ink, the words appeared on the page. Agnes continued to rub ink on the pages until she reached a page that only had two-thirds written on it. All in all, twenty-two pages had been written on in this fashion of invisibility.

"Now let's see what Franklin was up to," said Agnes.

Agnes skimmed through the pages. She read points of interest aloud to Harriet.

"Franklin found a diary in Salem that led him to Oozar in England. He wrote about studying various books and papers in the once-protected room at the London Library. This is where McDermit found Oozar's journal. Behind the worn, torn binding cover, he found the parchment with the heading 'Ofergīfre Onweald.' Franklin wrote the translation to be 'voracious power.' He described the symbol of the four elements. Here Franklin wrote 'roots' are the basis of the four principles."

"So where is this parchment now if it wasn't with this journal?" asked Harriet.

"Franklin wrote that Oozar went to 'Iseard' or 'Iceland' to collect three of the elements from the Surtsey volcano and the ice and the northern lights up on top of Vantnajokull Peak," Agnes continued.

Harriet asked, "What about the dying man's breath?"

"Franklin didn't write anything about Oozar collecting a dying man's breath. What Franklin wrote next describes in detail what James wrote to us about Oozar's skeleton being burnt up," answered Agnes.

Agnes continued to scan through the pages until she found the list of the four elements Franklin collected. He wrote in detail about how he bought the moon rock sample of the Genesis rock.

He also wrote that he caused the crash landing of the Genesis probe that brought back samples of the sun's solar flares. He also confirmed that he took the Antarctica ice and water samples.

Agnes read aloud, "The collection of a dying man's breath is Oozar's mistake. He collected not only the breath of life, but also the years of impurities that led to death. I conclude that the breath of life must be from a pure state, that of a newborn baby."

"That still doesn't answer the question of where the parchment is now," said Harriet.

Agnes read on, finding the answer. "He took the collection of elements to the cavern, including the parchment. Franklin is—or was—to blend the elements together, collect it into a hollow wand, and seal whatever it turned out to be inside."

"Oh, Agnes, you don't suppose he's—" Harriet started to say.

"At the séance, Grandpa said he is still alive," said Agnes. "We'll only know the truth by finding this cavern."

Chapter Twenty-three
My Trouble Has a First
Name and It's O-O-Z-A-R

The company party was coming up quickly. One problem did arise for some, teenage supervision. Agnes made sure the record books were happy and Robert hadn't caused any problems with the assembly line.

Agnes suggested to Robert to give him something to do that he should be on the company party committee. Robert, after all, was very good at negotiating contracts.

One problem had come up. What to do about Brian on the night of the party?

Agnes thought Harriet could have watched both Brian and Penelope.

"I know someone who could watch Brian," said Agnes.

"I'm not sure if Edna—" Robert started to say.

"You need to learn to trust me and the rest of us. We're not your Grimm's fairy-tale witches who eat children," said Agnes. "I have a thirteen-year-old cousin visiting from England who I will need to have supervised," stated Agnes.

"I'll tell Edna it will be fine," said Robert.

Agnes had another thought on her mind. She walked down the hall to accounting and went into Jay Münter's office.

"Excuse me, Mr. Münter," said Agnes. "By any chance are you having a problem with finding supervision for JayCee on the night of the company party? I do have someone to watch Brian Brown and Penelope if you need someone for JayCee."

"You should have checked with me first. I've been asked, and I accepted quite a while ago as someone's date to this company party," informed Harriet.

"And who would that be, Mr. Double-strength Love Potion with Pixie Dust Topper?" prodded Agnes.

"You know it's Winston. Since the faire, we have been seeing each other and actually talking," stated Harriet.

"Is that what you call it? Talking?" jabbed Agnes.

Penelope came in from spending the day with JayCee. She had showed him how to mix a potion for preserving spiderwebs.

"Anything I can do?" asked Penelope.

Harriet spoke up first. "You can find someone to watch three teenagers for the night of the Whitewing's company party."

"Who are the three teenagers?" asked Penelope.

Agnes said, "JayCee, Brian Brown, and you."

"I know someone," said Penelope. She pointed to the top shelf at the lamp. "He's really nice, and I'm sure he would be glad to get out of the lamp for a while."

"Oh, no," said Agnes. "He's the one who coined the saying, 'Be careful for what you wish for.'"

So Agnes tried Bee.

"Sorry, sweetie, the three of us have dates to this party. I'm going with H.G. White himself," boasted Bee.

The day before the party, Agnes pulled down the oil lamp and tapped it with her magic wand.

"I am the greatest genie of them all. Oh, it's you, Miss Candlewick," the genie said, disappointed.

"You don't do that bit for Penelope, do you?" asked Agnes.

"She likes my entrances," said the genie.

"I need you to do something," stated Agnes.

"Your wish is—"

"Knock it off and listen. I need you to watch three teenagers for six hours. You will not grant any wishes or promise them anything. If you cause any trouble, I will lose this lamp where no one will ever find it. In return, you will be allowed out of the lamp and eat food. Do we have a deal?" asked Agnes.

"Yes, Miss Candlewick. No wish granting. No trouble. No promising anything," said the genie, reluctantly agreeing.

JayCee was allowed to go over early with Penelope already being there. Agnes had let the genie out a little early to make sure he was ready for when the Browns showed up. Agnes had agreed for Robert and Edna Brown to pick her up as they dropped off Brian at the Hidden Quiddity.

"Put on some clothes," said Agnes. "And look more human."

"If you release me from the lamp, I will become my original self again, Miss Candlewick," said the genie.

"Not a chance. I don't trust you as you are now," stated Agnes.

Agnes explained to JayCee and Penelope, "Do not listen to him. Don't ask him to grant wishes. Be careful around Brian."

Winston walked through the door into the Hidden Quiddity. He wore a velvet crimson tuxedo and top hat. Everyone turned and admired him. Even Penelope couldn't take her eyes off him. Harriet came out of the back. She was wearing a blue silk gown with a matching wrap and clear glass shoes. She made her hair, lips, and nails match her gown. Strange as it seemed, JayCee found it very attractive for Harriet. Penelope couldn't help but notice that JayCee was staring at Harriet and felt a little jealous. Then she realized she had been doing the same thing with Winston.

Winston and Harriet walked toward each other without saying a word. They embraced, kissed each other, and disappeared. Agnes pulled out her wand and circled it around her head to change into what she would be wearing to the party. As the circle of light finished spinning around her, Agnes was dressed in a periwinkle dress with a cowl-neck, split flutter sleeves and an asymmetrical ruffled hem.

"That is a very lovely dress," said Penelope.

Agnes met the Browns at the front of the shop and escorted them quickly into the living area, which kept Edna from seeing too much of the shop.

"This is—" Agnes started to say.

The genie bowed and kissed Edna's hand.

"Lord Aryama at your service. What a lovely gown you are wearing tonight. You, sir, are also pleasingly outfitted well for the gala. Ah, Miss Candlewick, you do not have an escort tonight. I could—"

"No, thank you, Lord Aryama. I'm fine," said Agnes, stopping the genie from completing his sentence.

The Browns, along with Agnes, drove to the luxurious hotel on the other end of town where Robert brokered the deal of not only providing the ballroom, food, and drinks, but he also got everyone a substantial discount on hotel rooms for the night. People suggested he head up the annual family Halloween party that the Chamber of Commerce sponsored. A fifteen-piece rock orchestra, a comedian, and an illusionist who once traveled with a circus provided the entertainment.

The genie sat at the table where Penelope served pizza, what she found to be an easy magical food to make. He ate and ate and ate, along with Brian, who sat there and ate and ate and ate. Penelope made sure Brian had not seen her make the pizzas with her magic wand.

JayCee noticed the journal and papers were sitting on the table in the other room.

"Agnes found Franklin's journal!" he remarked.

"I didn't want to tell you about it until we were through. We have been staying up late working on translating and reading the journal for clues," said Penelope apologetically.

JayCee sat for the next two hours and read through the pages. He stared at the map of the area just outside of Broomstick and noticed the red circle around the cavern entrance.

JayCee went into where Penelope had been making the pizzas. "Any plans to go to this cavern?"

Overhearing the conversation, the genie said, "I can take you there."

"No!" said Penelope.

Brian sat there and paid no attention. He stuffed another slice of pizza into his mouth.

"You and I could go there tonight, take a quick look, and come right back. You could take us there with your dragon's breath," whispered JayCee.

"No, I can't. It is outside of Broomstick. Besides, Agnes thinks it's too dangerous, and we could get into trouble with her," she warned.

Disappointed, JayCee went back to the other room and picked up where he left off reading in the journal.

The genie walked in. "I used to be a great sorcerer before I became stuck in this lamp."

"If you were so great, then how did you get stuck being a genie of a lamp?" asked JayCee.

Penelope interrupted, "Watch out, JayCee. He may be a very nice person, but he was a sorcerer, and you can't trust him. He'll trick you into saying something that will be bad for you and good for him."

Disgusted, the genie went back to eating pizza and didn't say another word. But JayCee just couldn't let it go. He felt those feelings of needing to go and do something. They were stronger this time, as compared to the other instances. He really wanted to go to that cavern now. Penelope was in the other side of the living area. She had made more pizza. Brian was sleeping with a slice of pizza in his hand and food in his mouth.

JayCee felt a cloak of darkness had surrounded him. This was it. This time, the message was crystal ball clear to him. He knew what had to be done. He quietly sneaked into the potion shop. There, stacked neatly were brooms with uneven handles and straw that glittered like strains of gold. JayCee looked back behind him and made sure all was clear. He stepped out the front door and straddled the broom. It was like when he was younger and had played a cowboy.

His first instincts were right.

He said, "Fly."

The broom took off. Not too far behind him, JayCee noticed another person flying behind him. Penelope flew up on his right side.

Penelope yelled over at him over the noise of the wind, "Come back, JayCee! Please don't do this. Agnes will be mad."

But JayCee kept on flying. He ignored Penelope's pleas.

The waxing gibbous moon had given off just enough light that Penelope noticed JayCee's eyes were half-rolled back into his head. She saw JayCee's lips move.

But Penelope had only made out the words, "I must go and—"

JayCee flew down to the cavern opening. Penelope spotted the entrance and landed nearby. Out of his pocket, he pulled out some small sticks.

He held one up. "Torch."

The stick lit up. JayCee had grabbed them on the way out from a display that had a sign saying, "Instant light. Just say 'Torch.' Please do not light in the shop."

Penelope landed, knowing there was no turning back now. She followed JayCee into the cavern.

Robert and Edna enjoyed themselves that evening. Edna hobnobbed with other manager's wives while Robert was praised for having pulled off a great party. The committee had never done anything this good before.

Robert walked over to H.G. White. "Good evening, Mr. White. Good evening, Bee."

"Oh, you know Miss Bee, Robert?" asked H.G. White.

"Yes, sir, I do. She is my neighbor," Robert said. He leaned over to H.G. White, "You know she's a—"

"A hostess at the Poison Apple," he said. "I met her years ago when we merged with the Broomstick Company, and she still looks as young as ever."

Bee hugged his arm.

"I know this is a party, sir, but I thought I would show you this," Robert said, handing a contract to him. "An outside source has supplied this hotel for several years now. So, while negotiating for this party, I made a five-year deal to supply them with cleaning products from us."

"Well, this is a nice surprise, Robert," exclaimed H.G. White. "By the way, how are you doing over there?"

"I really like it, Mr. White. One of the best jobs I've had," he lied.

"Good. Good. Keep up the good work, and thanks for this surprise," H.G. White kept talking as he walked away from Robert.

Agnes was bored with the party. Harriet was having a great time dancing with Winston. So Agnes ducked out to a stairwell and disappeared. When Agnes returned, she headed straight over to Harriet.

"We got to go now!" stated Agnes.

"But it's not even midnight yet," complained Harriet.

"Now!" said Agnes.

She dragged Harriet over to the stair well and closed the door. Winston followed them across the room. At the stairwell door, he found one of Harriet's glass shoes on the floor. As Winston bent over to pick up the glass shoe, the clock in the ballroom chimed twelve times. Winston looked over at the big clock. The clock's hands pointed straight up to midnight.

Chapter Twenty-four
Jay's Assumption,
JayCee's Assumption

When Agnes left the company party for the first time, she went back to the Hidden Quiddity, the genie and Brian were sitting at the table asleep. JayCee and Penelope were nowhere around, and the map was missing. The second visit was with Harriet in tow. Agnes and Harriet changed out of their gowns and picked up their personal brooms.

It hadn't been hard for Agnes to track down two teenagers who flew basic flying brooms. The trail in the air was still warm, and Agnes's broom enchantment followed it right to the cavern entrance.

JayCee descended slowly down from the mouth of the cavern. He left a torch stick at the opening. As he got lower, water started to drip from the overhead, which had made the walking surface slippery. He came to two openings into other cavern rooms. Penelope watched her steps as she followed JayCee from the mouth of the cavern. She had barely caught up with him at the two openings.

"Which way do we go?" asked Penelope.

"To the left," stated JayCee with not exactly his tone of voice.

JayCee planted the torch stick at the left side and lit another one. The rooms were magnificent with large stalactites and stalagmites. There were calcium flows with soda straws that hung at the end with water droplets.

JayCee held up the torch stick. Penelope saw beautiful colors of white, browns, and coppers with streaks of blacks and grays in the calcium collections. As both of them stood at the entrance to the back cavern, Penelope noticed the room was smitten with black soot that covered the walls.

JayCee and Penelope saw a wooden table with bottles that had been sitting there for years and covered with a thick layer of dust. Under the dust was a large parchment paper. Through the dust, Penelope barely saw the ink writing. JayCee passed Penelope a torch stick. She lit it up and carefully inspected the bottle labels.

JayCee looked around the room as if he had been hunting for something he had lost. He noticed the floor had a burnt black circle with a white, ashen center. On one side of the black circle was a magic wand that lay between the wooden table and the circle. Over on the other side of the circle laid another magic wand. The one on the far side of the burnt circle pulled JayCee toward it.

JayCee heard in his mind repeatedly, "Pick up the wand. Pick up the wand."

JayCee stared at the magic wand. He walked over to the magic wand and stood over it. JayCee's eyes were aflame with a brilliant glow. A sinister smile had covered his face. JayCee bent down slowly and picked up the magic wand with the segment of the vortex trapped inside.

Penelope suddenly heard a loud crack. A flash of green light encompassed the cavern room. Penelope turned quickly to where

JayCee had been standing. A man with a long, black beard and thin arms with dry, brittle skin that poked out of a smoldered robe stood in place of JayCee. His eyes glowed red with black pools in the center.

Oozar spoke to Penelope in Old English, "You, my little witch, are going to assist me in my future endeavors."

Penelope kept her wits and asked slowly, "And how will I assist you with that?"

"As my servitude," stated Oozar. "You'll start by gathering up those elements and my parchment."

Just as quickly Oozar appeared, he was gone with a flash of light. JayCee lay sprawled on the cavern floor.

Agnes and Harriet landed next to the other brooms and found a torch stick had lit the cavern's entrance. Agnes led as the two climbed down into the cavern. They followed the footsteps of JayCee and Penelope. Agnes saw another torch stick was on the left side of the split cavern. The next area was dark.

Agnes pulled up the torch stick and used it to light their way. They heard a great echo of thunder and observed green flash up ahead. As they entered the area, Agnes and Harriet saw Penelope at the other end of the room.

Penelope faced toward them. A black figure had his back turned to them. Harriet reacted first and grabbed the wand out of the sorcerer's hand. With a flash of light, Oozar was gone. Harriet, Agnes, and Penelope stood over JayCee's body, which lay on the floor at their feet.

Agnes used JayCee's and Penelope's brooms to transport JayCee's limp body, along with the bottles, the parchment, and the two wands that were found in the cavern. Penelope rode on the back of Harriet's broom to the Hidden Quiddity.

The party got out about the same time that Agnes and Harriet arrived back at the potion shop. Robert and Edna drove over to the Hidden Quiddity. Agnes and Brian met them at the door.

"I came back early to make sure everything was okay. Other than a little too much to eat, he's fine," said Agnes, with a grimaced smile.

Brian climbed into the backseat of the car with a pizza-stained shirt and face to match. As the Browns drove home, Edna felt like she was back in New York, back on top of the social ladder. Agnes, on the other hand, had a thirteen-year-old boy who was passed out from a major diabolized possession, and the Münters hadn't shown up as of yet. The magical phone rang in Agnes' ear just at the right moment. Agnes thought this was the break she needed.

With tense lips and a nervous voice, Agnes answered, "Hello, Cindy."

"Oh, Agnes, I really hate to impose, but would it be all right if we picked up JayCee in the morning? We got a room here at the hotel for the night," said Cindy.

Feeling relieved for the first time since she had left the party, Agnes said, "It would be no trouble at all. Matter of fact, he is already asleep."

"Thank you," said Cindy. "You're a good friend to me."

Agnes sent Penelope to bed and laid JayCee in her bed. Agnes woke up the genie. He lazily swirled into the lamp. Agnes placed the magic lamp back on the top shelf.

"You're not angry, Agnes?" asked Harriet.

"What good would it do," said Agnes.

The next morning, Agnes woke up JayCee and got him ready to be picked up.

During breakfast, JayCee said, "I know you're very angry at me, Agnes. When I read the journal and saw the map, this feeling came over me. I had to go there right then. There was something there that I needed. I couldn't stop myself."

Agnes took hold of JayCee's hand. "I know the powers of Oozar's black magic possesses you. What you have told me before and what has been happening with you lately, he has been trying to get you to that cavern to retrieve that magic wand you picked up for years. My fears were realized last night. The power of Oozar is too great for us to overcome on our own. I now know how much trouble Franklin is in." She looked into JayCee's eyes, as if she were talking to Franklin. "I knew all along what must be done to stop Oozar, but I didn't want it to come to this. Three people almost lost their lives last night. She looked as if she hadn't had any sleep for a long while.

"In order for you to stop him, I must face a Witch's Council and be sacrificed?" said JayCee.

Before Agnes had a chance to answer, Harriet called from the potion shop, "JayCee, your parents are here."

Jay and Cindy stood in the potion shop. Jay was looking around at the unusual items for sale. Cindy already knew the whole truth and, more or less, accepted what she saw around her. Jay hadn't quite put the equation together just yet. He began to form questions in his mind.

Jay remembered what Robert had said about those people and the way he felt at the Poison Apple.

At the Hidden Quiddity, Jay, for the first time, connected the term "those people" to "Oh! Those people! Could they be … witches?"

JayCee came out from the back of the potion shop, ready to go home. Cindy nudged Jay toward the door before he could ask any questions.

"Thank you Agnes for keeping JayCee overnight," said Cindy, as she pushed Jay out the door.

"You know something about all this, don't you?" asked Jay when they were outside the shop.

"I know some things," said Cindy. "It's nothing to worry about. They're a little odd, but very nice people."

JayCee slept for a complete day and night. On Monday morning, he used his bicycle to go to the Hidden Quiddity.

"I'm going home early, JayCee," said Penelope. The corners of her eyes filled with tears.

"I'm sorry I put you in danger, Penelope. Franklin has been protecting me all these years from Oozar, and you gave me the power to resist him. I should have listened to you. I allowed him to possess me by picking up that magic wand. If it wasn't for Harriet, you and Franklin would have been dead," said JayCee. He held Penelope. Big droplets of tears were in his eyes.

"Agnes said it is too dangerous for me to stay here. She wrote my father a very long letter and sent it out by SNARF mail yesterday," said Penelope.

"What is SNARF mail? Can I use it to write you?" asked JayCee, sniffing back his tears.

"It's actually fairy-delivered mail. But, when you open the magical mailbox and hand them the letters, the fairies get all huffy about doing their job. They insult you and say nasty things about your letters. So it got the name 'Selfish Nerdy Arrogant Rude Fairy' mail. Your magical mailbox in your garden," explained Penelope with a half-smile.

That afternoon, JayCee and Penelope hugged each other and promised to stay in touch by SNARF mail. The warm air encircled Penelope. Then she was gone, like a dream you'll never have again. JayCee felt like someone had just socked him in the stomach.

"If this is love, I really don't care for it," JayCee thought.

He turned to Agnes. "Can we still be friends, Agnes?"

"Of course, JayCee," said Agnes, hugging him.

"Would you like to work for me here at the Hidden Quiddity until school starts?" asked Agnes.

"Boy would I," said JayCee.

"No magic whatsoever unless I say so," stated Agnes. "Now go sweep the floor with a sweeping broom." She laughed.

Harriet hadn't heard from Winston since the Whitewing Brooms party a week ago when she left early with Agnes. She talked to friends at the Poison Apple, and they said he hadn't been to work either. She went over to Winston's house, knocked on the door, and banged on the windows. Harriet tried various ways to get inside, but the protection charms were unbreakable.

"Harriet, it's only been a week," said Agnes.

"Not a word. Not one word from him," complained Harriet.

Winston had always been a mysterious person to everyone in Broomstick. He never told anyone where he came from or anything about his family. There was one rumor that Winston was a cousin of the Whetstone family, and that was about it.

As to the real reason no one had seen him since the company party (and no one would have guessed it), Winston went to face his parents.

Harriet was stocking shelves, and Agnes was helping JayCee with potion supplies when Winston walked through the potion shop door. He was wearing his velvet crimson tuxedo and top hat.

Winston walked over to Harriet and got down on one knee. From a pocket, he pulled out Harriet's glass shoe. Winston gently picked up her foot and slipped it into the glass shoe. Harriet was standing on one foot and put her other foot in the glass shoe while Winston held her up.

Harriet was magically transformed into her beautiful blue silk gown with her hair, nails, and lipstick matching the gown once more. Winston picked up Harriet in his arms, and they disappeared together.

Winston and Harriet were away for two weeks when Harriet appeared in the late afternoon at the Hidden Quiddity.

"Where did the two of you go?" asked Agnes, a little annoyed with the mystique of the situation.

"Ask me again some other time. Then I'll tell you. Right now, it's a secret I can't tell," said Harriet with sincerity.

The next day, JayCee observed a man in a black hooded robe with a golden cord holding it closed come into the potion shop. He wore a rolled brim pointed hat with stars and a crescent moon embroidered on it. Agnes, Harriet, and the man headed into the back of the shop and left JayCee to mind the front counter.

As the man passed JayCee, he stared intently. To JayCee, the man's facial expression was in between a frown and a scowl. It was almost really more of a questionable look then discernment.

After a half-day of being back there, the three of them emerged. JayCee noticed the man had the journal with the papers sticking of out it and the two magic wands that were found at the cavern. Shortly after the man left the potion shop, Agnes went out, leaving Harriet and JayCee alone at the potion shop.

JayCee put together a thought, "Agnes needed help to overcome Oozar's power. I must be sacrificed to stop Oozar from possessing me. Penelope left for home early because Agnes said it was too dangerous for her to be here. Now this man shows up and leaves with the journal and the two wands. He must be a very powerful wizard."

"Who was that man?" asked JayCee curiously.

Harriet looked at JayCee. "That was James Candlewick, Penelope's father."

JayCee had thoughts that spun like a tornado, terrifying him down to his bones.

"What is Mr. Candlewick going to do with the journal and the two wands?" asked JayCee.

"He is taking them for safekeeping and to study the matter of what to do," said Harriet quietly without any emotion in her voice.

"Does Mr. Candlewick know about Penelope and me?" JayCee asked, even though he really didn't want to.

"He knows more then we know about this whole mess. To answer your question, saying 'Yes, he knows' is way too short of an answer," admitted Harriet.

Agnes popped into Jay's office and pointed at the door. It closed quietly by itself.

"I'm having a little problem with the record books and transferring them to the computer program. I need you to come with me over to the production building," declared Agnes with a bewitched stare.

Jay sat there poised and looked at Agnes. "I'm not sure if I want to go over there with you."

"Then I can tell you why I am really here, and you will believe what I have to say," stated Agnes.

"How about you tell me first? Then I'll let you know if I believe you," said Jay with skepticism in his voice.

"Just a snap of my fingers and we'll be next door in no time," warned Agnes. She tilted her head down, and her eyes looked past her eyebrows. Her right one was higher than the left. She held up her fingers, ready to snap.

"Okay, I'll believe whatever you say," replied Jay, horrified.

Agnes removed any memory charms that had been put in place from years ago. Agnes told Jay who Franklin was and the reason why he had collected JayCee's first breath in a bottle. Agnes explained the unusual ability JayCee had because of Franklin's experiment. Agnes described the séance in unforgettable detail. She went into the description of the magical record books. Jay listened to how Franklin's journals and the map to the cavern were found in a private office. Agnes wrapped up the story with what happened to JayCee the night of the party.

"The only way to stop Oozar is by convening a Witch's Council. JayCee must be present since he is the connection to Oozar and Franklin. Tonight, I will be taking JayCee to where the Witch's Council is to be convened," said Agnes.

"Hold on. This is way too bizarre, and I don't think JayCee needs to go anywhere," exclaimed Jay. He gripped a pen tightly in his hand, like a weapon.

Agnes held up her fingers to snap.

"Wait … Is there another way to prove this to me? I really don't want to know what is over there," pleaded Jay.

"Tonight, when I come to pick up JayCee, you will have your proof," Agnes said.

She disappeared with a light poof of red smoke for a hammed-up exit.

Jay had gotten home before JayCee arrived from working at the potion shop. When Jay told Cindy what Agnes told her, Cindy just looked at Jay without any emotions.

Cindy said, "I knew most of it, except the part about JayCee going to the cavern."

"And you believed all this nonsense?" exclaimed Jay with heated breath and flaring nostrils.

"I was there when JayCee had one of those possessions," said Cindy. "Agnes and Harriet saved JayCee from the regular emergency room before they could do him any harm." Her voice grew louder and angrier as she spoke. "Don't call it nonsense until you know the whole truth," answered Cindy, with her hand clenched.

"The truth you say? You're saying that I don't—" Jay bellowed vociferously. Then he stopped in midsentence as JayCee walked through the front door.

Jay turned toward his son. His voice was dampened but still angry.

"I don't want you to go back to that shop ever again. I don't like the stuff they are filling your head with," Jay hissed through clenched teeth as he grabbed JayCee by the arm to escort him to the stairs.

But when their skin touched, flames encircled his hand and burned him like a blowtorch on a marshmallow. Jay pulled his hand back and screamed with agonizing pain.

A voice that wasn't exactly JayCee's spoke, "Do not ever touch me again!"

Cindy grabbed Jay, dragged him into the kitchen, and put his hand under cold water. The doorbell rang, and JayCee flung opened the door. He was confused and upset over what just happened.

JayCee waved his arms around hysterically as he blurted out what had just happened to Agnes. Agnes rushed into the kitchen.

Before she could say anything, Jay shouted out, "Is this your proof you were talking about?"

Agnes pulled out her wand and pointed at the sink. She began to chant a healing spell, "Bubble flutter butter churn. Heal the hand, and stop the burn."

Instantly, Jay's hand stopped hurting. He pulled it out from under the running water. His hand was normal except for the scar from the glass cut.

"Why don't you help out at the burn center?" asked Jay with an attitude in his voice.

"Magical burns can be healed with magic. That's just the way it is," explained Agnes. "JayCee, would you show your dad and mom the source of your power with a mirror?"

Puzzled, JayCee looked at Agnes. "I don't have a scrying mirror like you do."

"For this, any mirror will work, JayCee," said Agnes.

JayCee took his parents into the guest bathroom and stood in front of the mirror. He put out his arms and pointed at himself with his two fingers on each hand. JayCee crossed his fingers on his left hand. Penelope appeared in the mirror.

JayCee explained, "Penelope and I are connected by love. She is the source of my white magic that helps me control the black magic."

Then JayCee switched the fingers that were crossed to his right hand. Two wizards were in the mirror.

JayCee pointed out, "Franklin McDermit is holding back Oozar from completely possessing me. But his strength is weakening, and Oozar's black magic is taking over. In order for this to end, I must go with Agnes to face the Witch's Council. There is no other way."

JayCee dropped his arms and his head. While he looked down at his feet, he said in a caring voice, "I can't let Oozar posses me. If there is a possible way to save Franklin McDermit, then I must do what is best for all."

Jay and Cindy stood there and stared at their son in the mirror. Cindy had already accepted that there was a magical world and their son was a part of it.

Jay was still a skeptic, but he was reluctant to say anything against Agnes because of the threat of learning what was in that production building that had Robert scared of 'those people.'

"Come on, JayCee. It's time to go," said Agnes.

JayCee and Agnes walked outside. As Jay and Cindy watched their son leave, the two were swept up in a warming circle of air and disappeared into the night.

Chapter Twenty-five
The Witch's Council

In this magical community, there was a system of justice. When a witch or wizard had committed terrible crimes against the collective whole, a Witch's Council was convened, that is, if the witch or wizard happened to be captured, which made this a Witch's Council a very rare event. One hadn't been convened for centuries.

The accused witch or wizard was brought to the Altar of Blood and tied or chained to the stone table in the middle of a circle that represented the eight compass points. The judge stood at the north point. The jury of four took its place at the secondary points of the compass: northwest, northeast, southwest, and southeast. At the south point, hooded in the traditional mask that hid his or her identity, was the executioner. Two pillars of fire— one at the east and the other at the west—represented the sun. So as it was as, it will be evermore the Witch's Council of judge, jury, and executioner.

The eight festivals of the moon and sun were celebrated with music and food. They were the most magical times of the year. The most magical event of all was the rare and most powerful, the total solar eclipse. That was when the Witch's Council gathered.

That was when the abusers of magic were made accountable. A total solar eclipse must take place at the very moment of the Witch's Council.

At full totality, the executioner dismembered the guilty witch or wizard. The jury took the body parts and placed them in the pillars of fire. Thus was the sacrifice for the good of magic on the Altar of Blood.

This Witch's Council consisted of James Candlewick as the presiding judge. Harriet, Bee, Elizabeth, and Charmain were the four jury members. Agnes dressed in the executioner's robe and mask carried the execution sword.

The circle was assembled on Jenny Lind Island in the early morning. One more person attended this Witch's Council. James Candlewick, dressed in a black robe, stood at the north position while the pedestals and stone table were set up. Penelope Candlewick stood next to him. She was wearing the traditional Witch's Council witness ceremonial gown of green, translucent spider lace over a black silk-hooped dress with a black silk brimmed, pointed hat on her head.

When the stone table appeared in the center, JayCee was lying on it with the two wands over his head. The accused was normally tied or chained down to the table, but, in this case, JayCee was a willing participant in this trial.

Penelope realized it was JayCee on the stone table and exclaimed, "No, Father! I told JayCee I would not let this happen to him. There must another way to stop Oozar."

"Penelope, I have brought you here against your mother's wishes. I feel it's better for you to witness this than hide it from you," said James. "This will make you a better witch when you grow up."

After Agnes and JayCee disappeared to the Witch's Council, Jay turned to Cindy. "I have to see Robert Brown about who he calls 'those people' and his involvement in that production building."

"I'm coming with you," stated Cindy with quick conviction.

"The Münters just drove up," said Edna, peering out the window.

Before Jay and Cindy got to the door, Robert had the door open with the chain on it.

"What do you want?" asked Robert.

"I know what you mean by 'those people'. What I need to know is how did you find out, and how did you get involved with that production building?" asked Jay.

"I'll show you how I got involved with those people if you tell me how you got involved with them," said Robert.

Robert unchained the door and stepped outside.

He said, "Let's take a walk to the Poison Apple. I have some friends I want you to meet."

Cindy stayed behind to talk to Edna as Jay and Robert walked to the Poison Apple. Edna told Cindy of the three witches who lived next door.

"Did you see the young blonde hanging on H.G. White's arm at the company party? That is one of the witches who live next door. But she isn't young or blonde," gossiped Edna, referring to

Bee. "And those two hussies you know, they own a potion shop for 'those people' to buy their stuff for making spells to cast on all of us," continued Edna with a snooty attitude.

Then Edna said something that really upset Cindy. "You know that little girl your son has been following around like a beaten-down puppy? She's a witch also, and she has hexed your son into doing her bidding. Before your son, she tried to hex my Brian. But he was too strong for her and broke the spell before he could do anything wrong."

Cindy jumped up from her chair and pointed a finger at Edna. "I already knew she was a witch quite a while ago. But she did not, has not, nor will she ever put any hexes on my son, your son, or anyone else. Penelope is a kind, sweet girl, very proper and respectable. And, furthermore, Agnes is not a hussy. She is an upstanding business owner in the magical community, and she is a friend of mine." Cindy continued, not stopping for a breath, "And I would rather have a friend that is a witch then to be associated with a stuck-up, snobbish bigot like you."

Cindy walked out of the Brown's house and drove over to the Poison Apple. She felt quite proud of herself.

While Robert and Jay walked over to the Poison Apple, Jay told Robert about Franklin McDermit.

"JayCee somehow got magical powers because he collected his first breath and used it in an experiment," said Jay, still not fully understanding the whole situation. "Agnes tried to find McDermit over the years by watching JayCee and this magical power that was within him."

Robert told Jay about moving into this neighborhood by mistake and learning who they were and how H.G. White tricked him into that promotion to let him off the hook. Robert was careful not to divulge the secret of the broom.

At the tavern, Robert introduced Jay to some wizards who worked at the plant.

One of the wizards said, "You're JayCee's father. Nice boy you have. He'll grow up to be a fine wizard. And that English witch, Penelope, is a good match for him too."

Jay just stood there for a moment. "Uh, thanks. Yeah, JayCee is a nice boy."

Jay dropped the rest.

Everyone sat back down at a large table. Ale appeared in front of Jay and Robert. Chatter around the table consisted mainly of how the company had done and saying how Robert was a great production manager.

Jay mentioned in conversation, "I'm the chief financial officer of Whitewing Brooms. And honestly I really have no idea about the product line all of you are referring to. What are your particular jobs again?"

Winston was one of the wizards who had been sitting there. He described a new aeronautical flight pattern if the handles were curved a certain way.

Winston said to Jay, "We work on the original broom production line of the McDermit Broomstick Company."

"Oh, right. The one that, for unknown reasons, outsells all other products made by Whitewing Brooms," said Jay.

Jay had strange thoughts in his mind, "What does this broom have to do with flying techniques?"

That was when it hit Jay like a two-by-four square between his eyes.

"Straw into gold ratio, hand-braided rope manufacturers, stiltskins, nymphs, and flying techniques. They're making flying brooms over there in that building!"

Cindy came into the tavern and went over to where Jay was sitting. A chair appeared, and Cindy sat down, not bothered about where the chair had come from.

Jay leaned over and whispered, "You look steamed about something."

"Tell you later," she replied.

Cindy recognized one of the wizards from the company party. "Aren't you Harriet's friend?"

"Yes, Mrs. Münter, I am Winston Wisestone."

"Isn't Harriet a wonderful witch? And her sister Agnes is a good role model for little witches, don't you think? They both have been very kind to my son who happens to be magical as well," said Cindy in a loud voice.

"Cindy, what is going on here?" asked Jay.

But Cindy ignored him.

"Can I get a … Thanks," said Cindy. She picked up a drink that appeared in front of her. "Here's to new friends."

Everyone except Jay, until Cindy poked him underneath the table, picked up their drinks. They tapped glasses and took a swig.

Then Cindy asked in a loud voice for all to hear, "So who can tell me what a Witch's Council is?"

The whole tavern fell silent as the grave. Everyone stared at Cindy with a horrified look.

The time of the total eclipse neared. The trial had begun at first contact.

James spoke with a commanding voice, "You are accused of black wizardry for destructive personal gain. How do you plead to this charge?"

JayCee, laying stiff as a board on the stone table, spoke up in a loud voice, "Guilty!"

Penelope cried out, "No! Don't do this, JayCee!"

Again, James spoke, "And wreaking havoc against the wizarding world. How do you plead to this charge?"

JayCee, not moving a muscle, spoke loudly again, "Guilty!"

Penelope dropped to her knees as she cried. Tears ran down her cheeks.

James called out the last charge, "And possessing an innocent boy to achieve immortality. How do you plead to this charge?"

JayCee, cold dead and frozen laying on the stone table, spoke up for the last time, "Guilty!"

At the midpoint where the moon covered half of the sun, James called to the jury, "The accused pleaded guilty on all charges. What should be his sentence for these crimes?"

In unisonous, all four witches called out, "Death by execution and fire."

James grabbed and held Penelope back when she tried to get up. She wanted to run over to the stone table, but her father had made her stand next to him as he proceeded. Beads formed around the edge of the sun just prior to totality.

"Executioner, carry out the sentence as handed down by the jury," stated James with a cold, emotionless voice.

Agnes raised the sword over her head and looked up at the solar eclipse through the mask's darkened eyes.

"Now, JayCee!" Agnes yelled.

JayCee grabbed the two magic wands from above his head. The one with the vortex inside was in his left hand. He rolled off the table and faced James Candlewick with the two magic wands crossed over his head. Lightening sprayed out of the tips of both wands. He lowered the two wands down onto the stone table.

JayCee raised Franklin's magic wand over his head and slammed it down onto the magic wand with the vortex inside. Like a hot knife through butter, the hollowed-out magic wand was sheared in half by Franklin's wand. Crimson smoke bellowed out of the sheared wand and engulfed the stone table in a cloud of blood-red smoke.

Penelope screamed, "What's happening? JayCee? JayCee?"

She fell back down and cried with loud moans of despair. Disenchanted with what had taken place, Penelope clung onto her father's robe. The cloud rotated into a funnel cloud. The vortex opened. Quickly, Elizabeth and Charmain ran up to the stone table, and each grabbed half of the wand. They then headed toward the pillars of fire. As they placed the two pieces of the sheared wand into the fire, both pillars erupted with great fury.

More blood-red smoke bellowed out. Multicolored tongues of flames violently screamed of a man in anguish. As the fire burned out, the screams lessened in volume until no one heard them anymore. A bright beam of light streamed down onto the table into the middle of the vortex.

Agnes exclaimed, "The diamond ring!"

The vortex erupted violently with a storm of thunder. Something had fallen out of the vortex onto the stone table. The smoke cleared, and the vortex collapsed into itself as it disappeared into thin air. Lying on the stone table was Franklin McDermit, covered in soot and sweat.

Agnes dropped the sword and pulled off the executioner's mask. She ran over to Franklin, who was still lying on the table not moving.

"Franklin? Franklin?" cried Agnes, trying to pick him up.

"Agnes?" Franklin's dry, rough voice said.

"Yes, Franklin it's me. I told you I would be here whenever this moment would happen, just as I saw it in the crystal ball."

Franklin tried to get off the table, but he fell. Agnes wrapped her arms around Franklin and held him up.

"Don't turn me away this time, Franklin. I'm not a little girl anymore," said Agnes, holding him tightly.

Franklin balanced himself as he leaned onto the table with one hand. He wrapped his left arm around Agnes.

"I won't, Agnes. I won't," he affirmed.

Still not able to stand on his own, Franklin sat down on the ground and leaned his back up against one of the stone table legs as Agnes continued to hold him.

James walked over to them. "I still have unfinished council business to take care of."

Penelope held onto her father's robe, confused as to exactly what had taken place.

James pointed at Franklin. "I accuse you of wasting love when having predestined knowledge of who is your one true love. How do you plead to that charge?"

"Guilty as charged," said Franklin with a tired, dry voice.

"And you," said James, pointing at Agnes. "I accuse you of living with a broken heart and carrying this burden as if it were your fault. How do you plead to this charge?"

"Guilty as charged," said Agnes remorsefully.

Franklin asked, "Is it too late for us to be married?"

"It's not too late, Franklin. It is the right time for us," said Agnes.

"Then your sentence will be to get married and live happily together," said James as he showed some emotion of happiness.

Penelope found where JayCee had hid from the vortex storm after he slammed Franklin's wand down.

JayCee hid under the stone table, pale, frightened, and emotionally drained. For the first time in his life, he felt all alone inside. It was a disquieting chill that had JayCee frightened enough not to want to leave the sanctuary of the stone table. Penelope crawled under the table and sat with him. She took hold of JayCee's arm and squeezed it.

"I'm sorry, Penelope. I couldn't tell you what we were going to do. Your father came up with the plan to destroy the magic wand and remove the connection that Oozar had with me," explained JayCee. "Agnes also told me that, when I lose my magical connection with Oozar's black magical power, I would also lose my connection to you. I'm not a wizard, and I don't belong in your world."

"No, that's not true. I'm your one true love. Agnes even said so," pleaded Penelope.

Harriet leaned down and peered under the stone table. Penelope was holding onto JayCee's arm tightly. Cringing, JayCee moved away from Harriet for no real reason.

"Well, that isn't really the truth," said Harriet. "I did the tea reading, and it actually showed you would meet your first true love. I kind of misread it as one rather than first because we needed to get JayCee to meet us," admitted Harriet.

Agnes looked up at James from where she and Franklin had been sitting.

"I have a request of the Witch's Council," said Agnes. "I want to bestow magical powers upon JayCee and start a new family bloodline of wizardry."

James spoke with a strong, encouraged voice, "The judge and jury are in agreement. Your request is granted."

Agnes stood up and helped Franklin to stand up. He still needed to lean on the table, but he was feeling better. She motioned for JayCee to come out. He hesitated, but Penelope encouraged him with a gentle tug on his arm.

JayCee stood with Penelope as she held onto his arm and rubbed his hand with pixie dust from Sunshine.

"I can see there is real wizard within you, JayCee," said Agnes as she placed her grandfather's ruby amulet in his right hand and closed it. She wrapped her hands around his. "Grow up to be the greatest wizard in your family, JayCee."

Agnes then kissed JayCee on the forehead, which passed the amulet to JayCee. When JayCee opened his hand, the amulet was gone.

"This is now your magic wand," said Agnes, handing her grandfather's magic wand to him.

JayCee felt the surge of magical power all through his body as he took hold of the cordovan red, wooden magic wand. The emptiness JayCee felt earlier melted away. Another familiar magical connection had come back to him.

"I will also be your tutor," explained Agnes.

Harriet spoke up, "You'll have two tutors."

A whispered, strained voice interjected, "No, you two may assist in his learning. In order to learn to be a wizard, son, a wizard must teach you." Franklin continued, even though his words were less authoritative. "I will be your mentor, and you will be my wizard's apprentice. When I think you are ready, I will tell you when you are a wizard. Is this acceptable to you?"

"Yes, sir, that will be acceptable to me," exclaimed JayCee.

Agnes hugged Franklin tightly. Franklin took hold of Agnes. For the first time ever, he kissed her. Penelope hugged JayCee.

"I still want to be your one true love," said Penelope.

Except at the Renaissance Faire when they had first met, JayCee had never said it before in front of people. But, to JayCee, that didn't count.

"I love you, Penelope, and you are my one true love."

As JayCee hugged Penelope, Franklin moved his lips without making a sound.

"Kiss her. Kiss … her."

JayCee pulled away from their hug and looked into Penelope's beautiful, mysterious green eyes. JayCee put his lips together and kissed Penelope for the first time. JayCee felt a powerful magical force that surged through him and grabbed hold of his heart.

He had felt this feeling before from Oozar when he thought he was looking at Vigoda Whetstone. At that moment, JayCee realized love was more powerful than black magic could ever have been. Love was what JayCee based his magical powers on. With Penelope, he connected to it.

JayCee was Penelope's one true love.

CPSIA information can be obtained at www.ICGtesting.com
Printed in the USA
LVOW042358160911

246590LV00001B/22/P